THE SACRED VALLEY

THE SACRED VALLEY

Book Three of the
Rusty Sabin Saga

by

Max Brand

Skyhorse Publishing

Chapter One

White Horse stood at the head of the Sacred Valley. He did not know that it was the special domain of the great god of the Cheyennes, Sweet Medicine. He did not know that even the air of this valley was holy, feared of man. He only knew that there was peace unutterable between the cliffs on either side, and the gateway between towering rocks through which the river slid out into the cañon beyond. He knew that this was not like any land through which he had ranged in the days of his wild, free running, before the man had found him.

The grass was more dense, more richly green. The trees were rolling clouds, immensely large, and the very water had a snowy taste of purity.

Where in the world, besides here, could there be found buffalo ignorant of guns and therefore fearless in their numbers, or mountain sheep who grew pig-fat in the meadows of the lowlands, or tall mountain goats who forgot the heights to which they had ascended, since they needed no safety guards of high-climbing? Where could be found the herds of tall deer and the flashing disks of antelope who were also fearless?

White Horse lifted his head to the wind, which ruffled his mane and sent a silken flash through the length of his tail. On that wind he read the story of a thousand odors, and all of them told him of peace. His own sides were sleeked over a little with peace, even by these few days of resting in the Sacred Valley. His nerves were as still as the waters of the little lake just below the waterfall.

Above the chanting of the cascade he heard a thin, shrill, commanding whistle, small as the cry of a hawk from heaven. He shook his head and answered at a gallop. He turned into a white streak of speed that flung his tail straight out behind him, and so he came to the still margin of the lake.

There Red Hawk awaited him. White men called him Rusty Sabin, but he looked more like his foster fathers, the Cheyennes. And Red Hawk was also known as White Indian, because as a child he had been stolen by the Cheyennes and raised by them. As he sat on his heels, clad in only a breechclout, he washed the last pan of black mud. The eddy cleared the sediment away. With a quick, whirling motion he caused the cloud of soil to rise, to bubble over the side of the pan, and now the stream flowed, clear and free, into the dish. At the bottom there was a glittering remnant. He lifted the pan, poured the water out of it, and then into the cup of his hand transferred that remainder of golden bright pebbles and dust. It was very heavy. It was heavier than lead. He had washed more than $100 of virgin gold out of the lap of the earth in that single effort.

He poured the bright flash of it from one hand into the other, then he dropped the stuff into the mouth of the second buckskin sack. The other one was already full, and this one now was brimmed to the lips. He stuffed in a quantity of leaves, and then sewed the mouth of the sack shut, using for a needle the slender, curving end of a rib and for a thread a bit of the sinew of a rabbit.

After that, he saddled White Horse, who had been loitering around him, sniffing at the sacks, biting gingerly at the long red hair of the master. He snorted when the weight of the sacks was lashed to the saddle. How many other horses had carried $40,000 in gold on their proud backs? But White Horse preferred the living weight of his master.

Then Rusty Sabin — who all the Cheyennes knew as Red Hawk — pulled the moccasins onto his feet and tied about his waist the belt that supported the knife with the sixteen-inch blade on his left hip, the Colt revolver — that new and deadly weapon — on his right. To his own taste, the knife was the more significant weapon. He had made it in those old days when he had first been among white men. Now he had returned to the valley in search of gold and had found it. When he carried this load of wealth back and married Maisry Lester, he would settle down to a white man's life in some Eastern city, wearing hot, stiff, constraining clothes, a band of stifling cloth about his neck, polished and hard leather on his feet.

Every step that he took down the valley was a step toward the new life, a step away from the old.

He came to the mouth of the valley, the straight cliff on the oneside, the standing rock, like a huge fist, on the other. The river ran with a hiss of speed through the middle, and the big trees leaned out far, on either side, shadowing the water, leaving only a narrow trail on one side of the stream.

When he came to the mouth of the gorge, Rusty Sabin halted and struck a small fire.

He said in the Cheyenne tongue: "White Horse, lie down in honor of the Great Spirit." The white stallion instantly crouched like a dog. Rusty Sabin shook back his long hair and went on: "Sweet Medicine, I have come into your own house and taken something away from it. All my Cheyenne people think that this is very wrong. But I have come in under your eye. You see that I have not tried to steal anything away in the middle of the night, but I have remained day by day. I have killed none of the sacred cattle, the sheep, the goats, the buffalo. If you had been angry with me, surely you would not have taken the food from my hand. However, now I sit on my heels and talk with you, asking forgiveness for anything I have done that may be wrong. Give me a sign of favor or disfavor before I go away."

He listened through a long moment. There was only the soft, ominous murmur of the water as it fled through the entrance to the valley. And then, high above him, he heard the scream of an eagle or a hawk. Hastily he looked up. It was an eagle. It was an unhappy omen. And he cried out: "Sweet Medicine, are you sending me away like this? Are you giving me an angry word? Don't you understand that this is our farewell? I never shall be able to come again. Speak to me kindly before I go far away to my own white people."

He listened with a canted head, his hands turned up in supplication. But he heard nothing except the murmur of the sullen water. He stood up, at last, heavy of heart.

* * * * *

The white teepees of the Cheyennes, all made of the hides of buffalo cow, all well sewn, all well painted, all half sacred with the images that decorated them, rolled over a swell of the prairie not far from the bank of the stream.

As Rusty Sabin walked along, two miles away from the village, a crowd of the Indian boys on their wild ponies came racing, spied on him from a distance, and then charged down on him suddenly.

One of them carried a broken lance, leveled for mischief. Another had an old hatchet poised in his hands. At least three galloped with sharp arrows on the string, and every one of them had knives. So many mountain lions would have been less dangerous than this sudden flight of warriors-in-the-making, but Rusty Sabin walked straight on, without so much as lifting a hand.

That valley of young death came sweeping on until it was half a dozen paces away. Then it parted to the right hand and to the left. White Horse pranced a little and crowded up close to his master. But Rusty Sabin walked on through the dust that had been beaten into his face and gave no sign.

A sudden uproar broke out of the Indian camp. From it thrust a volume of mounted children, first of all, like sparks before the flame, and after them came thundering the whole warrior weight of the encampment, braves painted and unpainted, dressed or half naked, just as they had risen from *siesta*, or from a feast, or from the philosophical smoking of a pipe. Each of them had grasped some sort of a weapon, a rifle, a spear, bow and arrows; some brandished only knives, but as they came toward Rusty they shook the sky with their uproar. But chiefs with following or common warriors without distinction, all of them acted like madmen determined to kill their enemy if possible. Some dropped down along the sides of their horses and aimed arrow or rifle under the throat or over the neck of the pony. Others dashed straight in with hatchets raised for the kill.

But the whole crowd split to right and left and, with the howling of fiends, gathered again in the rear of Red Hawk.

Again only one rider rushed up to Rusty Sabin. It was a young chief with more than one red-stained coup feather in his headdress, and with a wide-bladed lance in his grasp. He landed on the bounding run, as the boy had done, and stood suddenly before Rusty Sabin, his hand raised in the air. He was a statue in gleaming copper, gloriously beautiful. He was in his early twenties, not a whit older than Rusty Sabin himself, and yet he carried himself with the unspeakable dignity of command.

Rusty leaped to the ground and answered that salute with a lifted hand, in his turn.

"*Ah, hai*, Standing Bull!" he cried.

Standing Bull could not speak for a moment. Therefore a sort of fierceness blazed in his face before he caught the hand of Red Hawk. Long before, they had mixed their blood together, and therefore he repeated the oath of the blood brothers.

"Your blood is my blood . . . my blood is your blood. Your life is my life . . . my life is your life."

Rusty Sabin spoke with him, word for word, and then they smiled on each other.

Standing Bull said: "If my brother has loaded his horse like a squaw coming back from buffalo hunting, let him put the weight now on this horse of mine. The pinto is good enough for Standing Bull, but Red Hawk cannot enter among the Cheyennes riding anything but White Horse."

Rusty, laughing, changed the precious weight of those buckskin sacks from the white stallion to the red bay of Standing Bull. On the back of White Horse he rode into the town of his adopted people.

Standing Bull, as the blood brother of this man, had taken precedence over the others, but now the rest of the warriors darted up close to him, one after another, shouting.

"Remember me, Red Hawk! There is a feast waiting in my teepee for you!"

Or: "Why do you listen to the others? I have fresh buffalo tongues and a squaw who knows how to cook them!"

Or: "I have a buffalo robe as soft as spring grass. Come to me, Red Hawk!"

Through these welcomes he rode into the inner circle of the camp and saw a tall form disappearing into one of the largest of the big teepees that made that innermost round. It seemed that the man was trying to escape to seclusion before the noise surrounded him. But as though realizing that he had been seen, the chief medicine man of the tribe now turned and lifted his face in a brief salute and gave to Red Hawk a fleeting glimpse of the tall, bent body, and the long face, placidly cruel, smiling with age.

Rusty Sabin rode past with an answering salute equally brief. A shudder far more lasting than the gesture passed through his body. More than once he had opposed Running Elk, and always victoriously, but there was something in his blood that told him trouble from that formidable brain lay ahead of him.

A girl flashed to the entrance flap of a teepee and shrank back again. In her place appeared a white man with a fat body and a bearded face, the beard formed toward a point at the chin not by trimming but by stroking with the hand. He wore glasses. And now he hurried out, waving his hand.

"*Ah hai!* Lazy Wolf!" called Rusty Sabin. Lazy Wolf was an easy-going white man, who had long made his home with the Cheyennes, and was Red Hawk's firm friend.

He jumped down from his horse and caught the hand of the white man. But he did not feel from this man the same slight chill that came over him when he greeted other whites of his own race. The skin of Lazy Wolf might be white, but his heart, like that of Rusty, was very largely Cheyenne. It was by his own choice that he lived with his red brothers.

"Come in, Rusty," he said. "Bring in Standing Bull with you. . . ."

"Go in with him," said Standing Bull. "I pass on to my teepee. When the feast is prepared and the best warriors have gathered to it, then you shall come to me, brother. But go in now with this other friend. He is a lazy man, but we know that he is brave. Peace to you, brother. While I am gone, remember me."

Rusty Sabin went into the lodge of Lazy Wolf, who closed the tent flap in haste after him.

"When you come," said Lazy Wolf, "you always bring a great dust with you." He turned to address the flashing-eyed girl who was his daughter by an Indian wife now dead. "Do you know why he stays away so long at a time, Blue Bird? It's because he wants the shouting and the cheering and the racing of horses, and the yelling, and the waving of hands with weapons in them. That's what he wants. So he never stays long. As soon as the shouting dies down, Rusty goes on again."

"Why do you speak English to him, Father?" asked the half-breed girl. "Welcome, Red Hawk. Here is a new willow bed for you to lie on . . . and if you grow chilly with the evening, here is a painted robe. Lazy Wolf paid ten horses for it! Isn't it beautiful? Here is a back rest. I made it all, even the feathering. Put your shoulders and your head back against it. So!"

"You see," said Lazy Wolf, "that she praises everything she offers to you as though she were about to make a sale to a trader.

Women are like that, Rusty. Confound them, they have to put a price mark on everything."

"Listen to them shouting for you, Red Hawk," said the girl, laughing with pleasure. "How they love you. Do you hear the squaws? There are babies born since you were last with the tribe . . . babies who never have seen your famous face. Go to the entrance of the teepee and let them see you."

"I can't do that," said Rusty. "I don't want to show myself like a little boy with his first tomahawk."

"You must go," she said, catching him by the hand. "There . . . stand up. Take this painted robe and throw it over your shoulders. Take this red pipe in your hand . . . here are some feathers for your hair. . . ."

"Hush. No, no," said Rusty. "I'll go, but I don't want to be decorated."

He picked up a doe-skin robe, light and soft and supple as velvet, and tossed it over his shoulders. Then he pulled back the entrance flap and stood before The People. The majority, now, were women and children. Behind them young braves sat on their horses together with a good scattering of more seasoned warriors who had returned to camp too late to see Rusty when he entered.

A great outcry came from all these people.

And, sure enough, a dozen women were holding up little laughing babies to look at the returned wanderer.

"Call the word to us. Give us the word! Oh, Red Hawk, call the word to us," the women began to chant.

He lifted his hand. A mortal silence passed over them. "I come from before the face of Sweet Medicine," he said loudly. "I have lived under the hollow of his brows for many days. He gave me peace and good hunting. I give it to you again, out of this hand . . . I pour it upon you . . . peace and good hunting." He dropped the entrance flap again.

Men and women and children were crying out with happiness. But Rusty sighed. He shook his head.

"How long I have been away," he said. "How very long. It seems to me that some of the faces are older, and some of them are missing."

"Why did you have to put the robe of that silly white woman about you, Red Hawk?" asked Blue Bird. "Since you went to live among the white people, have you become like them . . . ashamed of your body?"

"Perhaps I have," said Rusty. "I don't know. Things happen both to the mind we know and the mind we do not know. Among the white people, one changes every day. They are not like the Cheyennes, who never alter from father to son to grandson. They are a changing people. The red men are like the rocks that stand at the entrance to the Sacred Valley . . . ."

"Sweet Medicine, have mercy upon us," whispered the girl swiftly, automatically.

"The red men do not change, but the white men change . . . even the manner of the clothes they wear they continually are changing. The women know how to put on new faces every day. Everything there is strange to me . . . . Why should I be ashamed of my body? I am strong. I am not a cripple. And yet when I thought of facing the eyes of even the Cheyenne squaws and girls, I felt ashamed. That is all very strange."

"It is time for you to dress for the feast," suggested Blue Bird. "Do you hear them? Listen! Do you hear the war songs? All the braves are remembering their deeds in battle, now that you have come home. Ah, I wish I could be there tonight inside the teepee of Standing Bull and listen to the counting of the coups. Do you hear them singing about their deeds already? The hearts of all the young boys are aching, and all the warriors who never have counted a coup are sitting in darkness, with their heads down, praying for battle. That is because you have come home to us.

One brave man makes a whole tribe great. Because of one brave man, every warrior becomes a hero . . . the women bear bigger children . . . the children have hearts so great that they will not cry in the night. It is time for you to dress for the feast. Shall I dress you, Red Hawk?"

"Will you?" he said.

"Yes. But you never paint your whole body, do you?"

"No, I never do that. You know why."

She hung her head. "Yes," she murmured, "I know why."

He forced himself to say calmly: "It is still a pain to me to remember that I could not stand the torment of the tribe initiation. Perhaps Sweet Medicine sent that punishment on me. But of course it is too late to stand for the initiation again. If a lad fails once, he cannot have a second chance. But that is cruel. That makes the sickness in my heart, Blue Bird."

"Look," said Lazy Wolf. "The little fool is crying about it!"

Rusty touched her face.

"It is true! Your face is wet. What's the matter, Blue Bird?"

"I don't know," she said. "Nothing. But to think that you should have had such grief and shame . . . you . . . you . . . ah, Red Hawk."

"Go on," commanded her father. "Paint the red hawk on his chest, since that's all the ornament he'll have. Do it well, Blue Bird. You know how, by this time. I tell you, Rusty, that she's been painting the thing even on stones. At every encampment, on everything . . . always a red hawk . . . to remember you by, I suppose."

"Well, that's strange," said Rusty, "I'd think that you could remember a friend like me without painting a red hawk, Blue Bird."

"Ah," grunted the trader, "you never will have a brain in your head, Rusty."

The girl got out the paints and the brushes. She began to paint a pouncing hawk with wings furling back, and beak and cruel talons extended.

He bent his head and looked down to his chest. The wings of the stooping hawk extended right across his breast from shoulder to shoulder.

"How beautiful," said Rusty Sabin. "*Ai! Ai!* To think that I never shall be able to see it right side up."

"But you shall," said the girl, and brought out a square mirror that she held up before him, laughing.

He stared at the picture of himself, enchanted.

"And now you can dress," said Blue Bird. "Here are the whitest deerskin leggings . . . you see how they are fringed? Here is a shirt worked with porcupine quills of every color. Here are the beaded moccasins."

"Ah, how lucky if they should all fit," said Rusty.

"Lucky?" murmured Lazy Wolf. "Well, you may call it luck if you wish . . . but I'd call it foolishness."

* * * * *

In the lodge of Standing Bull the assemblage was so choice that not a single man was present who had not counted at least five painted feathers that represented the number of men each had killed — an honor far greater than the taking of five scalps. For that matter, it was known that Red Hawk never had taken a scalp in all the days of his life, but the smallest boys could not look on him without a shudder of admiration.

All of them were profusely painted in the most ceremonial style in whites and blacks and reds and yellows of fantastic design, so that they looked far from human.

Only Rusty Sabin himself carried on his breast the single design. By his failure, in his eighteenth year, to endure the tortures of the initiation into manhood, he had forfeited the proud privilege of being painted as a good Cheyenne should be for an important occasion.

The feast was short because the food was simple. It was washed down with water and, as a special luxury that showed the magnificence of Standing Bull as a generous host, with tea sweetened with sugar to the point of nausea. Rusty Sabin had lost some of his Cheyenne tastes. He barely was able to swallow that drink and keep on smiling.

Afterward, when the guests had departed, Red Hawk sat for a long time with Standing Bull and watched the dying of the fire. The son of the chief, excited by the strange events of the evening, whimpered now and then in his sleep, and the soft voice of the squaw hushed the child.

At last Standing Bull said: "How is it in your heart, Red Hawk?"

Rusty answered: "It is like a March day when the sun is bright and the wind is cold from the snow. I am Cheyenne, but I must go to live with my own people."

"Could you forget them?" asked Standing Bull.

"Whenever I look at the color of my skin, I must remember."

"Remember them, then, but stay with us. We have paid a price for you. A Cheyenne father has loved you . . . a Cheyenne mother has nourished you. The god of the Cheyennes has spoken to you."

"These are all great prices," agreed Rusty, shaking his head, "but my mother was a white woman, and the price she paid down for me was her life, which Dull Hatchet took, and her scalp, which the Cheyennes carried away."

"Does her spirit come near you still?" asked Standing Bull.

Rusty put his hand on the green scarab that hung from his neck. "You know, brother," he said, "that when the scalp is gone from the head, the spirit will not go to the Happy Hunting Grounds. Therefore her ghost is still wandering in the air. She is always near me. When I am with my people, the Cheyennes, I am glad, but she is unhappy. When I am with the whites, I am sad, but she is happy."

"If she paid down the price of her life," said Standing Bull gloomily, "then you belong to her and must do as she bids you to do. I am sorry for you, Red Hawk. How long do you stay with us now?"

"I go in the first gray of tomorrow's light."

"Ah, that is a sorrow for me. I shall ride part of the way with you, if I may."

"You shall ride with me, and bring with you ten of your best braves. Each of them shall take extra horses and saddles on which goods may be packed. When you return with them, there will be new rifles for all of the warriors who follow you. There will be some of the light woolen blankets that the white men weave with machines. There will be medicine against fevers, and knives of strong steel, and hatchets, and axes, and whole packages of beads, and eagle feathers, and everything that makes an Indian rich. There will be something for every man, and every woman, and every child in the tribe. You will stand in the center of the encampment and you will give out the gifts according to the rank and age of each. Every time you make a present you will say . . . 'This is from the hands of Red Hawk. In this way he says farewell to his red people.'"

"Are you so rich?" asked Standing Bull.

"I have been made rich by Sweet Medicine," said Red Hawk.

"Sweet Medicine have mercy upon me," murmured the young chief swiftly. "I shall ride with you in the morning, brother. But *ai, ai!* What an ache there is in my heart."

* * * * *

During the night the messages were sent. In the first gray of the morning, when even the dogs of the village still were asleep, twelve riders issued from the town and traveled across the prairies, each of them with ten or a dozen extra horses driven ahead in a swiftly running cluster.

They passed over the rolling country. They entered the lifeless flat of the true prairie, a green sea, a trackless plain where a compass would be needed for travel, or else the faultless instinct and memory of a red Indian. The prairie made them diminish. Within the immense horizon they grew leagues long, and man and horse became traveling specks.

Chapter Two

When the tap came at the kitchen door of the little house in Witherell, Maisry Lester was wrapping a blanket about her father. The weather was bland, but, as soon as the day ended, a dampness came into the air from Witherell Creek and the consumptive fever of Richard Lester was apt to begin again at that time of the day. So his daughter would start up the fire in the kitchen stove and make him comfortable again with a bit of warmth before he went to bed. There he sat with his head bent over a book while she hurried to answer the tapping at the door.

When she opened, Rusty Sabin stood there, laughing. But she shrank for a moment away from him. His suit of white deer-skin made his skin seem darker than the mere sun could dye it, and his hair was almost as long as it had been in the old, wild days when she had first known him. Besides, he was radiant with colored work of porcupine quills, like a fragile armor, and his feet glistened with an inlaying of beads. So she shrank for one instant as if from a wild Indian, then she ran into his arms.

He held her there, laughing. Her face was upraised, but he did not kiss her. That was a white custom that he had at last learned, it was true, but now he seemed to have returned to his old Indian ways, which did not permit of such intimacy. To any Indian a kiss was unclean.

He began to wave his hand over her shoulder to Richard Lester, Maisry's father, and Lester, shouting a happy welcome, started to rise.

15

Rusty ran and prevented him. Then he turned and called out in Cheyenne, and there appeared on the threshold six feet four of immensity — Standing Bull himself, with the fierce beauty of an Achilles on his face. The young chief carried in his hand a long-barreled rifle, and his other arm was raised to the ceiling as he said — "*Hau!*" — in a voice of soft thunder.

Rusty presented him.

"My brother, Standing Bull," he said. He chattered for a moment in Cheyenne.

The Indian turned his expressionless face to one and then to the other of the white people. His dignity was more perfect than that of a senator.

"Your brother, Rusty?" exclaimed Richard Lester. "You mean your foster brother, of course?"

"No, no. My blood brother. We have exchanged blood. We are the same flesh and the same spirit. Standing Bull is my brother . . . . Seat yourself, Standing Bull. Here is a chair for you. No, you'd rather sit on the floor, I know . . . . *Ah hai!* What do you think of him, Maisry?"

"I never saw such a man . . . does he understand a word of English?"

"Not a word."

"What shall we do for him?"

"Give him a dozen pounds of meat and he'll be happy. We've left ten Cheyenne warriors back in the hills with their horses. Standing Bull goes back with them in a few days, after they've had their presents."

"I have half a leg of cold mutton," said the girl. "What will he have with it?"

"Water" — said Rusty, then corrected himself — "no, tea . . . with plenty of sugar in it. A pot of tea and the sugar bowl emptied into it. That will make him happy."

Presently they had Standing Bull seated in a corner of the kitchen, with his rifle leaning against the wall beside him. On his knees there was a platter in which stood a gray crust of grease over the red of the mutton juice, and a great leg of mutton from which only one wedge had been carved.

Standing Bull got a good grip on the mutton bone, regarded knife and fork not a whit, and began to eat. He would sink in his teeth, get a grip on the long fibers of the meat, and then tear off a dangling strip that he consumed with snapping movements of head and jaw.

Both the girl and Richard Lester had to turn their heads from this spectacle, but while their smiles froze they saw Rusty regarding the huge Cheyenne with a look of the blindest affection.

"And that was what you found out of the great adventure? That was what you brought back from the return to the prairie, Rusty?" asked the girl.

He looked at the brightness of her hair and the blue of her eyes as though he could see nothing else. But presently he recalled himself and cried: "Ah, yes, there's another thing! Look . . ."

He ran out of the house and came back in a moment carrying a weighty little sack of buckskin. He was not a huge man like Standing Bull. Rather, he was made with a compact neatness and his weight lay only where it could be of the greatest advantage. And seriously or in frolic, there was not a man among the Cheyennes who cared to wrestle with that leaping, snapping, iron-handed, cat-footed Red Hawk. Now, with a stroke, with the side of his hand, he ripped open the sewing of the sack and dumped onto the table a flood of gold. Some of the nuggets rolled off the table and ran rattling to the ends of the room.

Standing Bull regarded that shining shower with only an instant of attention. Then he resumed his attack on the leg of mutton, which he rapidly was stripping to the bone. But the Lesters ran toward the table in one movement and spread out their hands to keep any more of the treasure from spilling onto the floor.

"Rusty! Rusty! Rusty!" cried Maisry. "What have you done? Where did you find it?"

"I didn't steal it," said Rusty. And he laughed to see their joy.

"Did you mine it yourself?" asked the father, his eyes burning as they gloated over the gold.

"Yes . . . I dug it and panned it all myself."

"If you got so much in such a short time . . . there must be millions left!" cried Richard Lester. "Where is the place, Rusty?"

"What do we care for millions?" asked Rusty.

"Care for them? Why, Rusty!" exclaimed the girl. "Do you mean that you wouldn't be rich if you could be?"

"It doesn't do much good," said Rusty. "If you have a great deal of wealth, your poor friends come and ask for it."

"But with us it isn't the way it is with Indians," she explained. "We don't give away all our money to beggars. Only something to charity."

"Is that all we do?" said Rusty. "Well, I've said good bye to the place where I dug that gold, and I don't think that I could go back. Not unless I were driven back."

"But listen to me!" cried Richard Lester. "Gold like this . . . free gold in such nuggets . . . great heavens, Rusty, it must be one of the richest deposits in the world!"

"Perhaps it is," said Rusty carelessly. "All that matters to me is that we'll have plenty of money now. I must go to work anyway, you say. Among the whites there's no free, happy life of hunting and war. There must be work, sitting at a table, writing on paper. And if it must be that way, then I shall make more money with my work. But this will take you wherever you need to be for your sickness, Mister Lester. And this will build a home for me and for Maisry. What more could a man want than enough? You know the saying among the Cheyennes . . . too much in the hand is the burden that breaks the back . . . . And there's an equal amount of the gold for my red brothers, the Cheyennes."

"*Ah ha?*" exclaimed Richard Lester. "An equal amount, did you say? For the red Indians? Rusty, are you going to waste a fortune on ignorant Indians?"

"Hush," said the girl. "That only will hurt Rusty's feelings. It's all right, Rusty. Whatever makes you happy is all right."

* * * * *

At the stores of the trading post, early the next morning, there was a murmur, a stir, and then a clamor. Here was a man ordering supplies at a rate that astonished them all. Four hundred rifles, with fifty-pound chunks of lead and solid poundage of the best powder, hatchets, knives for skinning, knives for cutting up meat, axes, spades, hoes in quantities, heavy packages of beads. Never had there been such a flood of orders delivered by a single voice in the town of Witherell.

"It's a war," said someone. "He's going to raise the Indian tribes. He's half an Indian himself, that Rusty Sabin."

But Charlie Galway, leaning on a long rifle, his curling hair sweeping across his shoulders as his head was bent in thought, remembered only one thing — that these provisions were being paid for in solid nuggets and in gold dust. Where that gold had come from, more could be obtained. And Charlie Galway was a philosopher who always thought past the present and into the future.

Among white men it would have been hard to find a more magnificent physical specimen than Charlie Galway. He was scarcely an inch shorter than Standing Bull himself, and, although he lacked some of the dimensions of the huge Cheyenne, he was almost as formidable about the shoulders. He had brilliant blond hair and blue eyes that turned to steel color, when he was excited, but he was rarely excited. This morning, looking up from under his brows, he watched the flash and shine of White Horse as Rusty Sabin moved the stallion back and forth. He looked at that bitless hackamore and watched the horse controlled more by voice and the touch of the knees than by the reins. He looked at the face of Rusty Sabin, too, and then turned to the man at his shoulder and said: "You know this Sabin? This fellow they call Rusty?"

"I know about him. Nobody really knows him," said the other. "How can you know a man who is two-thirds Indian? Not in blood but in brain."

"He's not big, but he looks like something," said Charlie Galway.

"That's what a lot of dead men say," said the other. "Fellows who have to shoot straight a lot of times generally manage to get the knack of it. He's had death in his face fifty times, I suppose. White Horse . . . that's the famous White Horse that you've heard so much about. Wild. The whole plains chased him for two years. Then Rusty Sabin went out and walked him down."

"Walked him down?" asked Charlie Galway, incredulous.

"Yes. That's what I said, and that's what I mean. Walked him down."

"Ah," said Charlie Galway.

Throughout the rest of the day Galway went on trailing Rusty Sabin, until the white Indian's great heaps of purchases were gathered together and paid for, all of them, in gold. And when but a double handful of the precious stuff remained, that went to a one-legged, white-faced fellow on the rim of the watching, envious crowd. A horse had fallen with him six months before; now he was waiting for death, rather than for anything that life could bring to him, until into his cupped hands Rusty Sabin poured those pounds of wealth.

And these were times when a lucky man might get 40¢ a day for his labor.

The cripple looked blindly down at the savings of a lifetime — at peace, at comfort, rained into his hands by heaven. He did not speak because he could not speak. And if he had had words, he would have addressed them to heaven, not to any mortal man like Rusty Sabin.

But Charlie Galway, watching, smiled a little, with the quick, flashing smile that goes with a secret thought.

Rusty Sabin might be a dangerous fighting man, but he also was a fool, and Charlie Galway was more than a match for any fool in this world.

Chapter Three

Ten Cheyenne warriors, silent, hard-faced, rode down into the town of Witherell and packed on the backs of their led horses the wealth for the tribe that Rusty Sabin had purchased.

"Where will the Sioux be now?" asked men who watched the procedure. "Where would Witherell be, either, if the red devils ever got it into their heads to tackle us?"

"They won't tackle the whites while Sabin is alive," said others.

Charlie Galway said nothing. He left the markets and followed Standing Bull and Rusty Sabin back to the Lester house. He followed at a distance through the evening, and as the day darkened into night he remained lurking in the vicinity.

Whenever anyone came near him, he was always seen walking briskly along. But afterward he would glide into one of the thickets that grew all the way from the crests of the surrounding cup of hills down into the streets of the village of Witherell.

When the darkness was complete, he heard sounds coming from the house of Lester, sounds of happy rejoicing — and then the enormous voice of Standing Bull raised in an Indian chant of triumph.

For Standing Bull was to spend this night with the Lesters and on the morrow he would return to his people, with his ten warriors and with the train of gifts that Rusty Sabin was presenting to the tribe.

What interested Charlie Galway more than anything else was that the windows of the little cottage had been darkened. Only points and lines of light escaped around the shades.

That was too much for Galway. He went down to investigate. There was no wind, which made every noise more obvious and increased the danger of his approach. But, also, it made it possible to pry up a window without having the shade fan out into the room. And when the window was lifted, he moved the shade aside just enough to take a view of the scene inside.

What he saw was enough to make the hair lift on his head. In a corner, curled up on one side and regardless of the noise in the room, lay Standing Bull, wrapped in a buffalo robe, sound asleep. For the hour of darkness was the usual retiring time for an Indian. And around a small center table sat Maisry Lester with such beauty in her face as though a special golden light were shining out of her spirit. And on the table before her and her father and Rusty Sabin was heaped raw gold, glorious gold, in dust and in nuggets.

Charlie Galway felt a stroke in his brain and in his heart. Destiny, he called it afterward. He heard a voice sounding inside him, and he would not resist the call.

That gold was meant for him.

They were weighing the treasure in a little balance scale such as a housewife would use in apportioning her cooking materials. And the sight of the gold fed the spirit of Charlie Galway to the lips.

They were weighing the gold, they were putting it bit by bit back into a buckskin sack. What a magnificent weight must be in that sack. What a joy to bear it. With such a burden he could have flown through the sky, he felt. He could have rivaled an eagle.

He went back and sat down under a shrub with his rifle turning hot under the grip of his hands. The stars drifted in the slow wind of heaven above his head; the voices died down inside the house.

Twice he was ready to start and twice he told himself that he must wait.

Then he went back to the house. When he rounded the place, soft-footed as a wolf, he saw that one light still burned — in the kitchen. Again from the window he peered in around the shade. And yet there was no wind to betray him.

He could see, now, the form of Standing Bull lying on the same side, as though he had not stirred a muscle since stretching himself on the floor. Richard Lester perhaps had told himself that he would sit by the failing heat of the kitchen stove until he grew more sleepy and his nerves were calm. A book was open in his lap and his head had dropped on his breast in sleep.

But there was in that room something that never would have allowed big Charlie Galway to close his eyes that night. Yonder on the table lay the little fat-sided buckskin sack of gold. Some of the precious stuff had not been brushed carefully off the table. A few bright grains of it sparkled under the lamplight that shone, also, over the blade of Standing Bull's tomahawk. This was simply an ordinary hatchet with an extra large head, but along the back of it ran a pipe stem to which a bowl and a mouthpiece could be screwed. In this manner the pipe of peace could be turned into a weapon instantly.

Charlie Galway grinned as he noticed that idea. It was after his own heart.

He felt that there had been an instinct, a fate behind this entire day, forcing him toward a definite destiny. And now he saw the thing before him — some $25,000 almost within the reach of his hand.

Once his mind was fixed, he abandoned all hesitation. He pushed the window shade aside, deliberately, and stepped in over the low sill.

The moment he was inside the room, the warmth of the atmosphere and the faint sweetness of cookery closed around him, breathing into his face. The very furniture in the room, the look of the walls, the worn, scrubbed floor were all friendly to the inhabitants and actively hostile to the invader.

He made two steps to the table and laid his grasp on the buckskin sack. His back was to Richard Lester, then, but from the corner of his eye he could see Standing Bull's sleeping face and the great, motionless arm that was flung out on the floor. The fingers of that hand opened and contracted slowly. There was a frown on the brow of the warrior. Perhaps he dreamed at that moment of battle.

"Galway!" gasped a quiet, startled voice behind the thief.

The right hand of Galway slid from the sack of gold to the handle of the tomahawk. Over his shoulder he had a glimpse of Richard Lester starting out of his chair with a horrified face. The book fell from the knee of the sick man to the floor with a crash.

And the nerves and the great muscles of the thief reacted with an instant violence. He whirled and struck as instinctively as a wild beast. The sharp, weighty head of the hatchet buried itself in the skull of Lester. He did not fall. He was crushed down against the floor by the force of the blow.

A harsh voice cried out from the corner of the room. Galway was aware, without turning his head, of a mighty shadow rising, and he plunged straight through the open window into the night.

Outside, he struck the ground running. Behind him he saw the bulky form of the Indian slip through the window to pursue, but at that moment Galway reached the brush. He dropped to hands and knees in the shadow there.

From that covert he saw the big redskin range to right and left, running with wonderful lightness and speed for a man of such bulk. The gleam of a knife was visible now and again in the hand of the warrior, and Galway crouched lower, his heart racing. He began to wipe his right hand on the ground. There was something wet on it, and he knew that it was blood. Had more blood spattered over his deerskins, a telltale symbol of the murder he had just committed?

Then, out of the house, a woman's voice began to scream. The shrill sound tore through the brain of Galway. There was no ending to it. He saw the big Indian go back through the rear door into the house. A fresh outburst of the shrieking started, on a higher note. Doors of adjacent houses in the village were slamming. Men were running, calling out to know what had happened.

Then Galway got up to his feet and circled out into the winding, irregular street that once had been a cow trail. Lights were coming on in various windows. The chatter of women sounded inside the houses. The voices of the men boomed with a hollow note in the open air.

He stepped into the shaft of dim lamplight that streamed out a window and studied his hands, his clothes. There were no spots that he could see.

He went back into the street. The screaming of Maisry Lester had ended, but the soft noise of her sobbing continued inside the house. There was a growing crowd of men outside the place. And big Charlie Galway walked into that knot of people. He could hear Tom Lorrance, that famous frontiersman, saying: "Who done the job? That's the main thing. Who done it? Who would smash in the skull of a poor fellow like Lester that didn't have any enemies?"

"There's an Indian in that house," said Charlie Galway. "There's a big, red Cheyenne Indian in there. Why isn't he the man that killed Lester?"

"You mean big Standing Bull?" asked Lorrance. "It ain't likely that he'd do such a thing in the same house where Rusty Sabin is."

"To hell with what's likely," said Galway. "He sure must've done it. Who but an Indian would murder a fellow like Lester? We'll go in there and have a look."

There was a muttering of assent. Instantly they started for the door of the house and Galway rapped on it.

Rusty Sabin came and pulled the door open.

"You can't come in, friends," he said. "Miss Lester isn't able to see people."

"We wanna see what's happened," said Galway. "We're the law and order of the town of Witherell, Sabin. There's been a murder done here, and we gotta know all about it."

"Is that right?" asked Rusty.

"Sure it's right," said several voices from the crowd.

"Walk softly, please, and don't speak loudly," said Rusty Sabin. "I'll go before you."

He paused in the hallway at a bedroom door that was ajar. He drew it shut, saying quietly: "They will be gone in a few moments, Maisry." Then he went on to the kitchen.

Standing Bull sat cross-legged in a corner, smoking. On the floor near the stove there was a dark stain.

"He must have been reading in this chair," said Rusty Sabin. "The murderer came in to steal that buckskin sack, because there's gold in it. He was discovered. He picked up the tomahawk of Standing Bull and struck down Mister Lester. There's the tomahawk. It was sunk clear into the head of Richard Lester. I took it out and carried him into a bedroom. Maybe, when the morning comes, we'll be able to find the trail of the killer."

"Takes it kind of easy, don't he?" muttered one of the men.

"Why not?" answered Charlie Galway, his hungry eyes on the sack of gold. "Fact is that it gets the cripple out of his way. I don't take no stock in that yarn about the thief coming in. How would a thief come in, anyway, without waking up the Indian or a man sitting by the fire? I tell you what, boys, this looks to me like a murder done by somebody in the house."

"In the house? You mean . . . one of the people in the house?" muttered another man, barely in the middle twenties but bearded heavily.

"That's what I mean," said Galway. He caught two of the men by the shoulders and drew them close. "Boys," he said, "I aim to think that stone-faced Standing Bull, yonder, is the murderer. He seen how much gold would buy, today. He seen the horses of his murdering, thieving Cheyennes loaded down with loot that hadn't cost any fighting. He seen his tribe made richer in one day with gold than it ever got through a hundred years of stealin'. So in the middle of the night he comes sneakin' to steal the gold. The old man sits there and sleeps. But he wakes up in time. He makes a holler. Standing Bull smashes in his head. But then, when he grabs the gold, it seems a mite too heavy to run away with. The girl comes in, sees her father dead, starts to screeching . . . . And so Standing Bull, he just stays here and faces it out. He says that he was asleep, too . . . stretched out on the floor, eh? Why, ain't that a lie on the face of it?"

"It wouldn't be a loss if we strung up Standing Bull by the neck," said Lorrance, nodding. "He's a friend to Sabin, but he's not a friend to any other whites. And he's got several hundred fighting braves at his command. He's the youngest war chief in the tribe and he carries a lot of weight. It'd be a good thing for us if Standing Bull was wiped off the prairies. It might save the scalps of a whole lot of white men."

"Maybe. But we won't do anything about it," grumbled big Charlie Galway. "We'll let him bluff his way right through. Inside his heart the Cheyenne is laughin' at all of us right now."

"I think he is . . . damn him," muttered Lorrance. "Why not take him out and string him up right now?"

"Watch Rusty Sabin," said Galway. "Watch that feller. He'll turn into a wildcat if you touch Standing Bull. They're blood brothers, people say. Here . . . Lorrance, you take after Standing Bull. Rush him sudden. I'll snag Sabin with this lariat. We're gonna have some justice done here in Witherell before the night gets much older."

Chapter Four

Lorrance said: "Sabin, there's been a right bad murder done here tonight, and some of the boys think that it was done by somebody inside the house."

"Someone inside the house?" repeated Rusty, staring, empty of eye and understanding.

"Yes . . . you, the girl, or Standing Bull. Leaving you and the girl out of it as not likely, that comes down to Standing Bull. We think that we oughta have a trial of Standing Bull. And a trial is what we're gonna have. Walk in on him, boys . . . Clary, take him from that side. Justis, grab him from the left."

Lorrance pulled out a revolver as he spoke. And, at the same time, big Charlie Galway tossed the noose of the lariat he had picked up over the head of Rusty Sabin.

That quick gesture should have taken Sabin out of the scene of action at once. Another man could hardly have resisted. But those long years among the Indians had given to Rusty that instant reaction of nerve and body that wakes a cat out of sleep when the teeth of the dog already are parting to catch her and puts her on top of the wall before the teeth have closed. Rusty shrank suddenly under the swift shadow of the lariat, and, as he shrank, the long, curving blade of his knife leaped out of its leather scabbard. As the noose dropped down over his shoulders, the edge of the knife flashed up and gashed it in two at a touch.

A glance over his shoulder told him that Galway had made that attack from the rear, but he had no time to think about

29

trouble from the rear. There was Standing Bull on the other side of the room with a rush about to start for him.

Rusty Sabin dived into the legs of that crowd like a fish into water and came up through a sudden confusion at the side of the gigantic Indian.

"*Ah hai*, brother!" shouted Standing Bull. "Shall we charge?"

He balanced over his head the long weight of his rifle, making it wonderfully light in the grasp of his huge hands, and the men in the room shrank back a little from him. They shrank still more from the look of Rusty Sabin, his red hair on end, his eyes a double dance of blue flame. The long blade of his knife already seemed to drip with blood, and in his left hand there was a heavy Colt revolver. All the tales concerning this strange fellow returned to the minds of the men of Witherell. One problem such as big Standing Bull was enough for them to handle. The addition of Rusty Sabin made the dish entirely a sour affair.

"Now what will you have?" called Sabin. "Is it a fight, or is it talking?"

"This is too bad, Rusty," said Galway. "You oughta know that we simply want to give Standing Bull a fair trial, kind of legal and everything. I knew you wouldn't understand, and that was why I tried to hold you back with that lariat."

"There's such a thing as law, ain't there, Rusty?" asked Lorrance.

"Yes," said Rusty. "That's true, of course."

He looked helplessly toward Standing Bull and said: "Brother, this is not a battle to be fought with the hands. It is a thing of law. And the white man's law never does wrong. They think you may have killed the old man. How can they tell that you are a great chief and that your hands are clean? But the law makes the truth appear. Even if we fight a way through them now, the trouble would not be ended. For such a thing, the white men would make war."

"Let them make their war," said Standing Bull. "The Cheyennes are ready."

"Ah, brother," said Rusty, "what do you know of the great cities and the tens of thousands of white men? There are more white warriors, all with good rifles, than there are buffalo on the plains. The Cheyennes are a great people, but when their bullets were gone and their hands weary with killing, there still would be white men by thousands and thousands. It is better to let the law wash your hands clean."

Standing Bull said: "It is very bad for a Cheyenne to take the law of the Sioux. Each people has a different language and a different mind. Their laws are different, too. White justice would not be Cheyenne law, brother."

"No, no," protested Rusty. "I have heard about this. Wise men have written great books about law. They have printed more words, Standing Bull, than there are blades of grass on the prairies. They have gathered together so much wisdom that they cannot help but be right. It is better to let the white men use their justice. It is much better."

"Brother," said Standing Bull, "I am in your hands. Shall I put down my rifle?"

Rusty said: "Wait still for one moment." He turned to the crowd of men. "Standing Bull will not fight to get away. He will stay quietly to be tried, because he is not guilty. But I have told him that white men have good laws. Will it be fair? Will you use only true laws for Standing Bull?"

"Aye, we'll give him a good chance," said Lorrance and Galway almost in the same breath.

Galway added: "Let's get out in the open. There's a moon coming up. We need more room than we got inside the house."

This was agreed to, and the crowd streamed out into the open street. It had grown, now, to include practically every man and most of the boys in Witherell, and at the windows of the adjacent houses appeared the women, looking on with a tense curiosity. The moon, newly up, was turning from golden to silver as it sailed into the sky.

There was a heavy wagon at the side of the street, and into this the Indian and Sabin were escorted. Galway said: "When you're up here before 'em, the lads can see what's what. You can talk to 'em better, Rusty. And of course you'll have to do the translating. There's nobody in the town that understands Cheyenne the way you do."

Rusty Sabin, looking over that crowd, found that his heart was falling every moment. Every man in that mob was armed, and there was a restless fierceness in their faces. Men did not come clear out to Witherell, on the edge of the prairies, except for important reasons. Here were long-haired hunters of the buffalo, and trappers who returned to the verge of civilization once every two years.

Down the street, at the head of the navigable portion of Witherell Creek, appeared the lofty twin smokestacks of the river steamer that was the link between the prairies and the inland regions, the huge water roads of the Mississippi Valley. Finally, a beautiful ghost in the pasture beside the Lester house, Sabin saw White Horse, gilded by the moonlight.

Charlie Galway stood in the foreground, calling out: "Attention, everybody! Here's Standing Bull, the great Cheyenne war chief. You can see that he looks young, but he looks mighty mean. What's the pleasure of you gentlemen about Standing Bull? Richard Lester has just been murdered in his own house. He was sitting in the kitchen where the Indian was sleeping on the floor. There's a noise heard. The other people in the house run into the kitchen. They find Lester lying on the floor dead, and Standing Bull is there, looking at him, and Standing Bull's tomahawk is sunk into the head of Lester. What does that look like to you, boys?"

One man stepped forward and flung into the air the noosed end of his lariat of rawhide. It dropped over the limb of a tree that stood beside the wagon and hung there, dangling, twisting a little like a dying snake.

"I'll give that much to justice!" he shouted. "The rest of you can string him up."

Instantly the nearer ranks of the crowd pressed about the wagon looking curiously and savagely up into the face of the chief.

"These people are not friends, and they are not fit to give judgment," said Standing Bull aside to Rusty. "Their minds are already fixed. Their thoughts are not like trees that grow, but like posts cut off and dead in the ground."

"You must be wrong, brother," said Rusty. "I have heard a great deal about the white man's law. The lariat on the tree is not to hang you. It is only a symbol of what happens to evil men. Tell me, now, exactly what happened in the house."

He listened for a moment, and, when the words were clear in his mind, he held up a hand for silence. The crowd gave it to him grudgingly.

"Listen to the white Indian!" called somebody.

Rusty Sabin said: "Standing Bull is my brother. We have mingled our blood together. He is an honest man . . . his tongue cannot say the thing that is not so."

"What are you trying to give us?" roared a man. "An Indian that won't lie?"

Rusty said: "Here is my right hand. The words of Standing Bull I would trust more than I would trust my right hand." Then he went on: "Standing Bull was asleep in the kitchen. He heard the old man cry out. He looked, and saw Richard Lester struck down with the tomahawk, which was lying on the table. He was struck down by a man who jumped out the window. Standing Bull drew out a knife and jumped through the window after the other. He ran here and there through the night. But there were many bushes and he could not see the murderer. Then he came back into the house. That is all his story, and it is true."

"That story ain't worth a damn," said a voice. And there was a loud murmur of agreement.

Rusty stepped forward to the edge of the wagon. "Who tells me that I lie?" he asked, staring over the faces.

And the sudden answer roared from fifty throats: "I tell you that the Indian lies!"

Galway leaped up into the wagon. Rusty caught him by the collar of his deerskin shirt and quickly drew his knife.

"Steady," cautioned Galway. "You see how the thing's running, Rusty? Now I'll tell you what I'll do. I'll try to change the mind of this here crowd, if you say the word. I'll talk them out of their idea, which is to hang Standing Bull right *pronto*. Listen to me . . . tell me where you dug up the gold and I'll change the minds of these people."

Rusty said: "The gold is in a place where no man can go."

"Where no man can go? Why, I'd go to hell and back for it," said Galway.

"Is this the white man's law and justice?" asked Rusty. "Is this all that they will do? Do they know who Standing Bull is? Do they know that he is a great chief and that he was a guest in the house of the dead man?"

"There's no use in you talking for him," said Galway. "You've said that you're his partner. They won't believe anything that you say. Speak up . . . will you tell me where the gold was dug?"

"Justice that is bought is not justice," said Rusty. "If I wrong a man, and then give him two horses, that does not make the wrong right."

"Get out of there, Charlie," said a man in the crowd. "And let's get done with the damned Indian. It's too cold to stay up all night."

"Will you tell me where the gold is, or will you let them hang Standing Bull?" demanded Galway angrily.

"What can I do?" asked Rusty sadly. "If Standing Bull dies, I must die with him. But if I tell you where the gold was found, my spirit and his spirit never will reach the Happy Hunting Grounds. There would be a curse on us."

"You damned ignorant, bigoted fool!" shouted Galway.

He leaped down from the wagon, and Rusty, looking beyond the crowd, saw White Horse, brighter than silver. He whistled. The stallion leaped over the pasture fence like a bird.

"Up and at them, boys!" shouted Galway. "A pair of damned murdering Cheyennes. Clean 'em up!"

"String 'em up in a pair!" yelled another man. "A white Indian is a pile worse than a red one."

Half a dozen men laid hands on the wheels of the wagon, preparatory to leaping into it. Others swarmed up on the tongue to climb in over the driver's seat.

And Rusty said to big Standing Bull: "Now, brother, I have been a fool to trust the white men. For the last time in my life I have trusted them. The Indians are far better. There is no white law so good as the Cheyenne laws of the tribe. If you die, I die with you. Strike together with me. Strike for White Horse!"

There was a general outcry, a sudden turning of heads away from the men in the wagon, for White Horse had come like an arrow toward the call of the master.

Since there was a throng of living creatures between it and the master, the stallion began to fight his way through with teeth and hoofs. And a sudden yelling and scattering in terror announced the progress of the big horse.

It plunged through an opening lane straight to the wagon.

"You first, Standing Bull!" shouted Rusty Sabin, and saw the Cheyenne leap far out and land safely on the back of the horse.

Rusty himself was instantly in place behind the chief. And White Horse, whirling, striking out with armed forehoofs, scattered the crowd before him as he fled.

There was a wild whirling of confusion, but the men of Witherell were not all handless and mindless in the crisis. More than one leveled revolver or rifle. Some failed to shoot for fear of striking down a bystander. And both the Cheyenne and Rusty had flattened themselves along the back of the stallion so that they showed little above the heads of the throng. In fact, they were clear of the fringe of the crowd, and with shouted commands Rusty was turning the horse toward the shadows of a grove of big trees, when the disaster came.

A dozen rifles had spoken, but only one bullet struck. Rusty heard the sound like that of a fist banged home against a soft body. He felt the shudder that ran through the body of Standing Bull.

Then the shadows of the trees received them.

He heard, behind him, the shouting of the crowd mingled with the furious or the agonized yelling of the men who had been injured by the teeth or the hoofs of the stallion.

Afterward he heard the drumming of hoofs begin, far behind him. He regarded them vaguely and dimly. For his arms were filled with the burden of Standing Bull as the big man lolled helplessly back, senseless, his head bouncing and jogging on the shoulder of Rusty.

And over the arm of Rusty flowed the blood of the Cheyenne.

Chapter Five

Fifty men came storming out of Witherell on the trail of the fugitives. In the midst of the hills they reached the spot where the Cheyenne warriors were packing their horses in haste. Those horses were formed in a compact circle, and the men of Witherell knew how many excellent new rifles were inside the living breastwork. The prize was rich, and they wanted their revenge.

But they remembered that Cheyennes fight to the death, and they remembered that Rusty Sabin was not a general to be despised. That was why they rode in great circles around the Cheyennes, yelling to one another, starting charges that never were driven home, and keeping the moonlit night echoing with their uproar.

Rusty Sabin, on his knees beside his friend, was working hard and fast to save a life. The bullet from the rifle had driven straight through the body of Standing Bull, and now the chief lay muttering, murmuring, making no sense with his words. He had lost much blood. Now the wound was carefully bandaged and the bleeding had ceased — outwardly at least — but his body was shuddering with a fever.

When Rusty pressed his ear to the breast of his friend, he was sickened by the weak, rapid fluttering of the heartbeat. The life of Standing Bull was on the wane. Would he live till the morning?

A horse litter was arranged quickly. Two tender saplings were cut down and fastened at either end to the saddles of a pair of horses. The central point between was wrapped thick and soft with buffalo robes, and on this bed the warriors laid their chief.

He still was muttering and murmuring, and every sound of his voice wrenched at the heart of Rusty Sabin.

The little caravan was ready to start now. He arranged the pack horses in short columns, tethering them to the war ponies that were strung out in a central line. And there in the core of the moving body the Cheyenne warriors rode with rifles balanced across the bows of their saddles. Slowly the little group started forward. And Rusty Sabin on White Horse rode behind as a rear guard.

The men of Witherell had not gone home. When the Indians started to move away, they raised a great shouting and commenced to follow. More men had come out from the town. There might be a hundred of them, all told, but they were not ready to risk a headlong charge against those Cheyennes.

A living bulwark of horseflesh lay between the braves and the attack, and every man in Witherell knew that Rusty Sabin had taught the tribesmen how to shoot straight.

They might sweep the Cheyennes away in one tumultuous charge, but, if they did so, they would be sure to pay two or three heads for one. So the riders from Witherell flooded here and there to the rear. They set up a fresh shouting when they saw Rusty Sabin drop back behind the caravan.

He began to ride up and down, and, as he rode behind the main body, he shouted a challenge that ran clearly back to the ears of the white men.

"*Ah hai! Ah hai!* Do you hear me? White men, do you hear? I was Sabin. I was one of you. My skin was white, also. But you took the blood of my friend and with it you dyed my skin all red. I am no longer white. I am a red man. I am Cheyenne from the heart to the eyes. I never shall come among you again except as an enemy. I give up my part of white blood. I am all pure Indian. I am Red Hawk, the Cheyenne. Do you hear me?"

A loud yelling answered him. Half a dozen of the riders plunged suddenly forward. He lifted the butt of his rifle to his shoulder and waited. The charge split away and recoiled while it was still at a distance.

"*Ah hai!*" shouted Rusty. "Are you afraid? Little house dogs, why do you bark so much? Have you smelled wolf?"

A shouting of fierce anger stormed up from the riders of Witherell. Again there was a sweeping movement forward, and again the charge dissolved, recoiled.

"Look!" shouted Rusty. "I am a Cheyenne. I call to you, dogs! Will you answer? Let three of the strongest house dogs come and try their teeth on a wolf of the prairie. Are you all cowards? Are you afraid to come?"

Here and there the men of Witherell had gathered in little knots. But White Horse shone in their eyes like silver and the fighting name of Sabin dinted their hearts with equal force.

No pair or trio rode out against Rusty Sabin.

He shouted: "Now I know what you are . . . dogs, and the sons of dogs! If you come near the Cheyenne lodges, we will send out the dogs with whips to beat you home again. Murderers! Traitors! Without clean tongues, without truth, without honor. Dogs, dogs, dogs! Listen to me again. I was to marry a squaw from among the white people. Tell her that my heart is sickened. In the house of her father Standing Bull was a guest. And the house dogs gathered and sank their teeth in his flesh. Now I forget her. I shall have no wife but a Cheyenne. I shall raise my sons to scorn the white men. And when we want white justice, we will come and buy it by the pound like traders. You that have no god, no honor, no faith, no manhood, but you deny me . . . come down body against body and fight me, and Sweet Medicine strike on my side against you. You will not come? Farewell! I turn my back. I leave my scorn behind me. I go back to the good life!"

* * * * *

They passed out of the Witherell Hills, and on the verge of them the angry men from Witherell turned and rode back toward their town. Those riders from the trading town reached the place again in the early dawn, and it was long-haired Charlie Galway who went with Lorrance to the house of Maisry Lester.

Some women from neighboring houses had come in to prepare for the funeral. Charlie Galway and Lorrance found Maisry herself, white-faced but steady. In the pale morning light the brightness of her hair seemed to shine with a glow that came from inside it.

Her voice was quiet and even, but she went straight up to Lorrance and said: "Is it true? Have they driven Rusty out of Witherell? Did they shoot down Standing Bull and drive Rusty away?"

Galway said: "This is mighty unpleasant to talk about. But the fact is that Rusty went sort of crazy. He went native, Maisry. There ain't any other way of saying it. Went red Indian and told all the whites to go to the devil."

"All the whites?" she asked.

Lorrance said: "Sorry, Maisry. He went clean crazy. He howled out that he never would come near whites again except with a gun. And he'd marry a Cheyenne, he said, and raise his sons to take white men's scalps."

"You take it from me." Galway nodded. "You're mighty well out of it. You and him might've started happy, but in the finish something would have turned him into a crazy Indian again. He's got it in him. He's got it in his blood."

She got to a chair and slipped down into it. Her head fell back and her eyes stared up at the ceiling.

"Take a bit of this whiskey. It'll brace you up," said Galway.

She shook her head.

"It's a mean business," agreed Lorrance. "You tell us what we can do for you."

She shook her head again.

Galway started to speak, but Lorrance took him by the arm and pulled him out of the house.

Galway said nothing. He was looking away with distant eyes of thought, building already a new scheme, far greater and more sweeping in its scope than the last of his inventions of the mind.

Chapter Six

When the dawn came, Rusty stopped the caravan. As the procession moved on, it was impossible for him to tell whether Standing Bull lived or died. Now, leaning over the litter, he stared into the half-opened eyes of the chief. There was a film across those eyes. A cry of agony started up into the throat of Rusty, reached his teeth, and stopped there.

He leaned and pressed his ear against the breast of the warrior. Nothing? No, after a moment he could make it out — not a heartbeat but a mere fluttering like that of distant wings. Was the spirit leaving at this moment?

He made a fire with wood chips. Over it he cooked a broth of dried venison. He took the head of the chief against his shoulder and fed him the soup in small swallows. Some of it ran down from the loose mouth and spilled on the scarred breast of Standing Bull. But some passed down his throat, also. His fever had diminished. His body was cold. Rusty wrapped it in two robes. He listened first to the heartbeat and found it stronger, more steady. And hope rushed into his heart like a bird into the sky.

Later in the day, he arranged a shade to keep the force of the sun from the face of Standing Bull.

At every halt he made a small fire and after cleansing body and spirit with the sacred smoke of the sweet grass, he prayed to Sweet Medicine. But all day long the god gave no answer.

When they halted at night, he lay at the side of the motionless body of Standing Bull to give him warmth. All night long he was awake, praying in a faint whisper, throwing his thoughts up toward the moonlit sky, begging from Sweet Medicine some sign of success.

The morning came, and at dawn he felt the body beside him turn cold.

He heated more broth. Standing Bull could swallow. At last he opened his eyes and the fever was gone from them for a moment. "Are we dead souls or living, brother?" he asked.

"We live, Standing Bull," said Rusty.

The Indian smiled and fell instantly into a deep sleep.

They went on again, the caravan making many halts. And at last, far away, they saw the hills turning the edge of the sky to blue, like so many low-rolling clouds. Later, the hills turned brown. They discovered a glint of shining white — the teepees of the Cheyennes. And now three chosen braves rushed their ponies off to announce that the treasure train was approaching — and that the wounded war chief of the tribe was coming.

That announcement struck through the encampment like thunder ringing around and around the great throat of a bell. A joy and a fear seized on every Cheyenne of the camp, a joy for the plunder and a fear for the life of Standing Bull. For he had proved himself as great a leader as he was young. He carried victory in his hand.

He had brought in a rich harvest of Pawnee scalps.

There was only one man in the camp who would rather have had Standing Bull dead than alive, and that was Running Elk. The old medicine man hated the war chief not so much for his youth as for the affection that bound Standing Bull to Red Hawk. The white Indian was the consuming hate of Running Elk. More than once the mysteries of Running Elk had fallen to nothing before the strange cunning of Red Hawk. In a time of famine, for instance, it was obviously proper to make medicine first and go hunt the buffalo next. And yet while Running Elk was making medicine, Red Hawk had slipped away with a small band of followers, found buffalo, and returned with horses laden with rich stores of fresh meat, to the confusion of all the magic of Running Elk. Worst of all had been the matter of the treatment of disease.

The legitimate practice consisted of much dancing and smoking, much howling to the spirits, much fasting, leaping, running to the point of exhaustion, and finally a fat fee to the medicine man; sweat baths were the order of the day in every illness, and, although the sweat baths very often killed the patient, sometimes the sick man survived.

So Running Elk, when he heard that Red Hawk was returning with so many horses loaded with treasure — and with the sick war chief in hand — leaned his cruel old chin on his fist and began to think. And the more he thought, the more he smiled, so that his squaws looked at him with shudderings, for they knew what his smiling portended — trouble, great trouble.

The procession came into the camp in silence — a tribute to the illness of the war chief. But it was a silent joy when the braves had a glimpse of the treasures that were being transported in the packs. Only Running Elk remained apart, and smiled his smile, wrapped to the eyes in a painted buffalo robe worth the price of half a dozen good war ponies.

He went to visit the sick chief, when Standing Bull was laid in his teepee, smiling weakly with happiness to be home again. And, leaning over him, Running Elk stared intently into the dull eyes of the wounded man. He knew something about the eyes with which death first looks out of the face of man; he knew that the chief was not half a step removed from the end. And a thrill of hope ran through the body of Running Elk. Hitherto, Red Hawk had worked wonderful cures. Yet he had been these days with Standing Bull, his own brother by blood ceremony, and had failed to heal him. Did it mean that Sweet Medicine at last had turned his favor from the white Indian? Was it not clear that a touch would kill the war chief now?

Running Elk went back to his teepee and pondered his thoughts again until a turmoil began in the round central clearing of the camp, just before his lodge. He went out and found the tribesmen gathering to receive the distribution of the gifts. Running Elk stepped into the center of affairs at once.

He got on a horse and made a speech that was brief and burning. He said: "Brothers, I have prayed. I have received wisdom. This is what the Sky People say to me. They say . . . 'Running Elk, go among the warriors. Tell them that they make themselves happy at the thought of riches, but they forget that their war chief is almost dead. He is almost dead because we are not pleased with them. He is about to die because all the Sky People are angry with the Cheyennes. So let us see what the people are willing to sacrifice to us. And if they sacrifice enough, we will let Standing Bull be cured.' This is the way the spirits talked to me. And I tell you, my friends, that it would be wise to take half the packs of the horses that were brought to us from the white men, and burn the treasure. Let us see if that is sacrifice enough, and let us not touch the rest of the treasure until we are sure that the Sky People are happy and pleased with us again. We shall know, surely, by the sickness or the health of Standing Bull."

A gloomy groan answered Running Elk. But it was a groan of assent.

A prairie Indian did not lie to his fellow tribesmen. To an enemy, to a white man, a lie was far better than the truth. Many a lie told in the camp of an enemy was as famous in Cheyenne tradition as great deeds in open battle. But among friends, the truth had to be told. That was why Running Elk was believed. He said that the Sky People had talked to him, and therefore the Sky People must have talked. They demanded a sacrifice, and therefore a sacrifice must be made.

The logic was simple. A war chief should mean more than treasure. If the sacrifice of treasure would make him well, then of course the sacrifice should be made.

It never occurred to a single man in the tribe that Running Elk was a malicious old liar. The only one who saw through the thing was Lazy Wolf, the white man, but he was an outlander who never interfered in tribal affairs.

For too many years he had watched the odd workings of the Cheyenne mind and he now stood by with a queer smile and watched the boxes of rifles broken open and heaped in a stack, and the good powder poured over them, and the axes and the hatchets, the excellent knives, the cloth, the bright beads, and everything up to one half of the heavy horse loads that had been carried all the way from Witherell across the hot prairie.

And then the fire was set. The powder burned up with a tremendous flare. But it did not explode. It had been mixed with enough earth to prevent that. The heat of the fire was tremendous, because a good core of firewood had been provided. And so $10,000's worth of trade goods went up in one tremendous flare.

The braves watched with impassive faces, but there was murder in their hearts.

Afterward, still gloomy, they listened to the medicine man as he said: "The sacrifice has been made. In the morning we shall see if the Sky People have been pleased."

Then he went back into his lodge and told his wives to permit no noise within the lodge, for he would be communing with the Sky People from that time forward. He raised a mighty stench burning magic herbs and sat contentedly in the middle of the smoke. For his heart was happy and hopeful.

And the next morning, Lazy Wolf strolled into the lodge of Standing Bull and saw Red Hawk seated cross-legged beside the sick man. Blue Bird kneeled behind Red Hawk, murmuring at his ear: "You are very tired. You are so tired that your eyes have turned into the eyes of an old man. Lie down and sleep. I will watch beside Standing Bull. His wives will watch, also. If you don't sleep, Red Hawk, you will grow sick and die. If you kill yourself, will that make your brother well?"

Red Hawk put out his hand and laid it on the arm of Standing Bull. The chief was sleeping, muttering in his sleep. But at the touch of his friend he grew quiet at once.

The two wives of Standing Bull laid their fingers on their lips and looked at each other in wonder. They had watched the touch of Red Hawk work this marvel before, but they never ceased to delight in the strangeness of it.

The pulse that Red Hawk was feeling was very irregular, very weak. It never had stopped that horrible fluttering that promised every moment to end, and with it would end the life of the chief. Standing Bull was much altered. The fullness of his lips had diminished. There was a blue shadow in his temples. His eyes were sunken, although no more than the eyes of the man who watched beside him. The flesh was falling away from his cheeks. His breathing rattled through partly opened lips.

Red Hawk, making no answer to the girl, looked with indescribable anxiety on the sick man. More than once he had tried to lie down and sleep, compelled by the agony of exhaustion, but always he was prevented by the horrible thought that now, perhaps, in that moment when he was off guard in slumber, death would steal the spirit of the chief.

Lazy Wolf murmured: "While you're sitting here, do you know that Running Elk has persuaded the fools to burn half the treasure you brought out to them?"

Rusty, without a word, rolled back his head and looked up with the red-stained eyes of sleeplessness at the face of the trader.

"That was yesterday," said Lazy Wolf. "And this morning, when they heard that Standing Bull was no better, they've decided to burn the other half of the things you gave them. Running Elk eggs them on . . . there . . . you can hear the spitting and rushing of the fire. There goes the rest of the treasure, Rusty."

Rusty closed his eyes and took a breath. He had thought that the greatness of his gifts might be a thing for these red people of his to remember. But that hope was gone.

He shrugged his shoulders and looked at the death-like face of Standing Bull again.

"Well," said Lazy Wolf, "the fools won't help Standing Bull with all their sacrifices. But why don't you get some sleep? Here . . . let me look at you. You're more than half sick yourself. Is it true that you haven't closed your eyes since you left Witherell?"

Rusty looked away from the questioner. He had forgotten that the trader was there. And Blue Bird, rising, took her father by the arm with both frightened, anxious hands.

"You have a wise brain. You must do something. Standing Bull may live, but Red Hawk will die if he continues like this. His eyes are terrible. Have you seen them?"

Red Hawk muttered, just audibly, turning up the palms of his hands in prayer: "Be merciful, Sweet Medicine. His blood is my blood . . . my blood is his blood. His life is my life . . . my life is his life."

Blue Bird began to weep silently. And her father tried to take her from the lodge, but she said: "I must stay. If he faints, I'll give him some of the ammonia, as you told me. And if he dies, I don't want to live."

"You are young, and all young girls are fools," said Lazy Wolf calmly. "Red Hawk won't die, but he may drive himself crazy with all this watching."

"Will Standing Bull get well?" she begged.

"Rusty is doing all that every doctor in the world could manage," said the trader. "Standing Bull ought to be dead before this, but, since he's lived this long, the chances are that he'll get well. There'll be a change for the better before very long, and once he starts getting well . . . why, I know how tough the Cheyenne stock is."

"But Red Hawk is not Cheyenne, except in his soul. He is killing himself, Father."

"Young men take a lot of killing," said the trader. "If you want to stay here and enjoy the suffering, do it. I won't prevent you."

And he went off, whistling.

It was not long after that that the frightened squaws of Running Elk fled from the teepee and stood about it, holding up their hands to keep passers-by silent. So a speechless crowd began to form in a pool about the lodge of the medicine man. Strange howlings, growls, beast noises, human screams issued from the teepee.

And the squaw explained: "Running Elk is listening to the spirits. The Sky People are telling him things that he doesn't want to hear. Listen to him shouting to keep their voices out of his ears. It is something about Red Hawk."

The crowd had grown large before Running Elk came to the entrance of his lodge and pushed the flap aside. He stood leaning against the horse post, with his head sunk on his scrawny old chest, in the attitude of perfect despair. Several of the older warriors came toward him, but they moved slowly, unwilling to come too near to one who, obviously, had been wrestling with the powers of another world.

"What is it, Running Elk?" asked a scarred chief. "What have the animal voices told you?"

"I tried to argue and fight against them," said Running Elk in a husky, feeble voice. "But what can even a medicine man do when the Sky People have made up their minds? This is a sad day for the Cheyennes. Standing Bull, I am told by the spirits, cannot get well unless Red Hawk is put in the Valley of Death, and the mouth of the valley guarded until he is dead."

Running Elk turned with a groan of despair and disappeared into his lodge.

Then his voice could be heard by the silent, stricken people outside as Running Elk said: "Save your servant, Sweet Medicine. Save Red Hawk from death. Lift him in your claws. Carry him out of the Valley of Death."

In the medicine lodge itself gathered all those warriors and old men who, in the course of their lives, had counted five notable coups. Near the central fireplace of the lodge sat Running Elk, the palms of his hands upturned, his face raised, as he prayed continually to the Sky People.

The warriors, hooded to the eyes in buffalo robes, listened silently to the medicine man. At last, when he made a pause, an ancient brave stood up and let his robe fall to the hips.

"Running Elk," he said, "why should the Sky People wish to send Red Hawk to his death in the valley? If we lose him from the tribe, we have lost our greatest warrior. Who else has counted so many coups? Who else has brought us so much good weather? Who has healed so many of our sick?"

"I listen," said Running Elk, in his saddest voice, "and the Sky People say to me that they are unhappy. They cannot turn their faces toward the Cheyennes, because in the tribe they see honor and the first place given to a man whose skin is white, and to a man who could not endure the fear and the pain of initiation.

"The Sky People love the Cheyennes, but they are ashamed when they see Red Hawk among us. That is why they let Standing Bull lie weak as a woman, dying. They say that Red Hawk must die. Each of you has a white stone, and each has a black stone. Drop whichever you will into this bowl. The black stones mean death."

They stood up in order, the oldest first, the youngest last, and one by one went to the big earthen bowl near the fire, each dropping in a stone, while Running Elk sat by, praying in a soft voice continually: "Sky People, begin to look at us again. We have sacrificed many things to you. We pray to you every day.

We pray now that we may do the right thing and please you. Do not break our hearts with misfortune. We know that it is better for one man to die who is not of our blood than for all the tribe to be in misery."

He did not end his soft-voiced but audible praying, until the last stone had been dropped into the bowl. And when he looked down into it, he had to bite his thin old lips to keep from smiling. For nearly every stone was black. There were not enough white ones to make the entire mass seem grey.

The medicine man stood up, gathered his robe about him, and said grimly: "The voice has been heard. Red Hawk must die."

Chapter Seven

They came in a small procession, with heads downward. Running Elk remained outside the lodge of Standing Bull. Four of the most prominent veteran warriors of the Cheyennes entered and one of them laid a hand on the shoulder of Rusty Sabin. He looked up and saw the face of the brave painted black.

"Is it war, brother?" asked Rusty huskily.

"It is death, Red Hawk," said the brave. "The Sky People have spoken. They have spoken in a clear voice. You must go to the Valley of Death before life can come back to Standing Bull. You must go so that the Cheyennes may become a clean people again. My heart is sick and weak like the heart of a woman, but the Sky People are our fathers. We must do as they bid us."

Rusty Sabin stood up in a trance and left the lodge, walking past the frozen face of Blue Bird, the stricken fear of the two squaws of Standing Bull.

In the open air, he found the bright sun flashing on the silk of White Horse. Exhaustion made all the background of the scene whirl before his eyes. He mounted the stallion; the warriors closed about him; the procession started with the braves holding their war lances reversed, the points sloping back toward the ground as they would have carried them if returning from battle in which a great war chief had been killed. Except for the escort, Rusty saw only one face as they rode from the camp.

All the others, even the women, even the children, suddenly turned their backs when they saw the solemn cortège, but

Running Elk showed his face with the cruel, placid smile of age upon it.

One flash of rage and clear understanding entered the befogged mind of Rusty, as he understood to whom the Sky People must have spoken. But all the way from the camp to the Valley of Death his weary brain was benumbed, and his tired body kept sinking to sleep. He was in fact drowsing on the back of the stallion with lowered head when the procession halted and many strong hands helped him to the ground.

He looked around him with a clearing brain. He remembered the place. Every Cheyenne had passed it with a shudder of cold flesh. It was not half a mile from the entrance of the Sacred Valley on which he alone, of all men, had looked. And this gorge, cleft in the same tall hills, was the exact opposite of the flowering green of the Sacred Valley. For here no river ran. It was a box cañon, surrounded on all sides by impregnable walls hundreds of feet high. It was a bottle from which no man ever had escaped once the narrow jaws of the entrance were blocked.

To this place Indians who had lost the savor of life and wished for death often came. Here they entered, killing their horses at the mouth of the terrible ravine and taking the oath to give themselves to the Sky People. Across the entrance lay the whitening skeletons, the long bones, the horrible, dark-eyed skulls of the dead horses. And inside, men said, were the skeletons of hundreds of Indians who, in the course of the ages, had come to die in this place.

Nearly all were voluntary suicides, but now and again the tribe would pick out some culprit who had proved himself a danger to the people and escort him to the Valley of Death.

He looked up. Inside the entrance gap, he saw the naked shimmer of the cliffs in the sun, and high against the thin, sunwashed blue of the sky he saw three small blots of darkness circling — buzzards wheeling over the charnel house. They were proof that something had just died in the valley, or else with prophetic instinct they knew that something was about to die. Tales were told of the horrible birds beginning their feast even before the last glimmer of life was gone from horse or dog or man.

"Here is your knife, Red Hawk," said the oldest of the braves. "With one stroke of this you may kill White Horse at the entrance to the valley and so make sure that your spirit will be well mounted for the Happy Hunting Grounds."

Rusty took the knife. He stripped saddle and bridle from the stallion. He raised the blue sheen of the curving knife blade toward the sun.

"Listeners above, listeners underground," he said. "Out of the wilderness I took White Horse. He has carried me to famous deeds. As far as the name of the Cheyennes is known, White Horse is known also. I return him to the places from which he came. Go!"

With that, he slashed the lariat that was noosed around the neck of the horse and flung up his hands. The stallion wheeled in sudden fright, and fled away, turning himself into a glimmering streak with his speed until he was lost from view among the great rocks that were scattered over the plain at the mouth of the gorge.

There was a brief, deep outcry from the Indians who watched.

"Brother," said one of them, "will you let your poor spirit wander on foot through the sky forever?"

And Rusty answered: "I gave him love as much as he gave me. I give him freedom now as much as he can take and keep. My friends, I am sorrowful only a little bit. If my life could be held in my hands, I would spill it on the ground willingly to bring back the life of Standing Bull. But I know that this cannot be. He needs prayer, but, also, he needs rest, a cool lodge, and food. These things you will not give him. It is not the will of the Sky People that drives me away from my tribe. It is the howling of an old, skinny dog, Running Elk. He has told lies, and my people, like children, believe those lies. I am not angry. I am not afraid. But I look at your faces and sigh. You seem to be men, yet you have only the brains of babies."

He turned his back on them and walked through the entrance without once turning to look back; he merely could hear their murmur of astonishment and anger behind him.

He was walking into a new world and he was equipped for it with only a single weapon — the long, blue-bladed knife of perfect steel that he himself had hammered into shape and tempered so that it would take and hold a razor edge.

The bones of the dead horses he picked his way over and came to the full view of the Valley of Death. It was as naked as its name, a sun-scalded place of rocks. Here and there a talus of broken debris had slipped down from the faces of the perpendicular cliffs, but except for these aprons of rubble the high rocks were unapproachable. And here and there, on the dark rocks of the cañon floor, he saw white chalk marks — and he knew that those were human skeletons bleached by the suns of a hundred summers. He walked on.

A shadow seemed to strike over him from the cliffs. It was the sleepiness of the most intense exhaustion. There was a patch of sand between two rocks. He sank into it. It seemed to him that a dark influence arose to him out of the ground. If this were death, it was delightful. His eyes closed. He slept at once.

The day closed over him. The chilly morning came. He wakened when the sky was flaring with rose and with bright gold. He stood up and thought for a moment that he was standing in the blue fields of the Happy Hunting Grounds. Then he realized that he was only in the Valley of Death. Out of the distance, voices were chanting a morning prayer to the Sky People, faintly, and he knew that these were the Cheyennes who had brought him to the place and who were now guarding the entrance. For seven days they would guard the place. Then they would go away, knowing that their man was dead.

Seven days? Already thirst pinched his throat and burned in his forehead. The sun rolled up a swift, bright wheel over the eastern cliff and instantly the valley was filled with fire. He gave one searching glance to the terrible cliffs. They were impregnable. So he prepared to die quickly. He took out the great knife and looked down the sheen of its blade. It seemed to Rusty Sabin that he could understand now why he had made that knife with such loving care. It had been to make easy the taking of his own life, in the end.

The heart or the throat? If he put the keen point under his heart and tapped strongly on the butt with his free hand, death would come as quickly as the wink of an eye.

He lifted the knife to the heavens and chanted the briefest of death songs: "Here am I, Red Hawk. My skin is white but my soul is the red of a good Cheyenne. In my life I have kept my word. I die because my people will it. Sky People, is this thing what you wish? Answer me!"

It seemed to Rusty that he could hear a faint answer, although that was doubtless the echo from the face of the cliffs.

And again he sang: "There are only four faces I leave behind me. I say farewell to Maisry and Blue Bird, to Standing Bull and Lazy Wolf . . . and I say farewell to all my people, when the white smoke goes up from the lodges on a winter morning . . . when the spring mist covers the teepees with thin blue . . . when all the children laugh and sing in the river . . . when the prairie is red with the blood of buffalo. Sky People, is this the thing that you wish? Answer!"

Again, more clearly, he heard a voice. It was no echo, and, turning about in great excitement and fear — for even at the moment of death it was terrible to hear a voice from the spirits — he saw in the distance the figure of an old man who sat cross-legged on the ground and smoked a pipe.

That picture of peace amazed the mind of Rusty utterly. This might be any one of the powerful ghosts from the underworld or the region above the sky. This might be Sweet Medicine in a new guise. Rusty went with reverent steps toward the figure. When he was close, he saw that it was a man of immense age, bent and shriveled by time to the size of a child. Rusty raised his hand and gave the greeting. But the stranger smoked on, watching him with bright little curious eyes.

He took the pipe from his mouth to say: "What is your name on earth, or are you not a ghost?"

It was good Cheyenne that Rusty heard, but not the speech of his own tribe among that nation.

"I am no ghost, father," he said. "My name is Red Hawk."

"Are you the rider of the white horse?" asked the other.

"I am he," said Rusty. "I shall ride White Horse no longer."

"Why are you sick of living?" asked the Indian. "You still have strong legs under you and a good pair of hands. You can strike in battle, take scalps, count coups, dance, boast, sing, look at pretty young women, and fill your belly with plenty of stewed buffalo tongue in summer, and plenty of good pemmican in winter. Why should you leave the world?"

"The lies of Running Elk sent me here," said Rusty. "He persuaded the people that I was their bad fortune. They brought me to the Valley of Death."

"A medicine man," said the Indian, "is always jealous. Running Elk was jealous of you because you were a fool."

"Why was I a fool?" asked Rusty.

"You were a fool," said the Indian, "because you tried to be not one thing but many. You have a white skin, but you call yourself a Cheyenne. You are a warrior, but you became one without the pain of the initiation. You are a wise chief, and yet you had to be a medicine man, also. A man should be one thing, not many."

"I suppose so," said Rusty. "And who are you?"

"I have had several names in my time," said the other. "I have been called Long Lance and Red Answers The Blow, and several other honorable names after battle. But The People remember me better by my name as a boy. Young Spotted Calf is what they used to call me."

"Spotted Calf, I have heard of you."

"Of course you have," said the old man, "and that is why I am ready to die and hungry to die. All the Cheyennes have heard of me. I am therefore living more on their tongues than in my flesh. There is more weight in the words of the young men when they sit at the fire and tell of my deeds than there is weight in this dry old body of mine. And then the other day a horse kicked me and smashed some of my ribs. Why should I pay many horses from the herd to the medicine man to have my bones cured? I would not pay them. I took the oldest horse from my horse herd and traveled toward the Valley of Death. The horse fell down and died yesterday morning. I came on and reached the Valley of Death about noon. And so you understand why I am here?"

"Spotted Calf, it is a pity when such a famous man as you leaves his tribe and his family. My heart aches for the Cheyennes. They need your wisdom."

"I was never very wise," said Spotted Calf. "When I was a young man, I used to puff out my chest and tuck in my chin and make speeches, using all the good-sounding words. But my speeches never made very much sense. When I grew older, I used to sit with the elders very silently. If there was a question to be discussed, I never said a word until all the others had decided. Then I would say one thing. Sometimes a single word. And even the old men thought I was wise. If a man is willing to listen, other people always think that he is wise. Then I grew older still. I grew so old that children began to look at me with eyes of fear. When I saw this, I knew that I was too long among my people."

"Spotted Calf, you are an honest man," said Rusty. "If I could find a way, I would save your life and my own."

"My own life is lost, now," said Spotted Calf. "The fever and the pain of the broken ribs is in my blood. It will not come out again. You see?"

He pulled his robe aside, and then pushed down a loose bandage that girt his body. The flesh along one withered side had been torn loose from the ribs. The whole wound was horribly infected.

Rusty sickened as he stared.

Spotted Calf knocked the ashes from his pipe and looked down at the wound. "I am decaying, you see," he said calmly.

"What can I do to make you comfortable, father?" asked Rusty.

"Nothing, my son," said the old man. "Nothing except to go away for a little while. The pain is growing great, and now, as you see, I am as weak of soul as an old woman. I wish to have a few moments for groaning and sighing. Afterward, like a woman delivered of a child, I shall be quite content again . . . or dead. But it is a pity that death has to gnaw so slowly at an old, dry, useless bone like me. Even death, that wants all things, does not want me now. Farewell for a little while, my son."

And Rusty walked slowly away. He felt that life had been defined for him in a new way. And with this new definition it was not worth having.

Chapter Eight

There was one thing he should have asked the ancient chief. He should have inquired what it was that made the old man call out to him. For it seemed to Rusty, more and more, that the voice had been in direct answer to his call. He had put his question to the Sky People, and a voice from the ground had spoken to him in reply. Should that be interpreted as direct intervention from the sky?

Rusty went to a distance so that Spotted Calf could, if he wished, groan like a very woman. From the stone on which Rusty sat, he could see half a dozen skeletons on the rock. Some of them were totally disjointed, so that they looked like white writing on the stones, a language that only the Sky People could understand.

Thirst was growing a more and more fierce torment in the throat of Rusty. And the fatigue of his long watch at the side of Standing Bull left him still weak, still with a glaze before his eyes.

A thin shadow flicked over him. One of the buzzards had stooped not a hundred feet above his head. It sailed with a whisper of wings straight across the valley and alighted on a tall rock. There it sat perched, half spreading its wings as though to rise again, and thrusting out its horrible long, red, scalded neck as it stared downward.

Rusty started to his feet. Behind that rock old Spotted Calf had been seated. Then a sudden thought sent Rusty running toward the place.

The buzzard hesitated, thrust out its head to stare at him, then rose with clumsily flapping wings, struck them aslant with a sudden ease through the upper air, trailing its foul shadow again over Rusty.

When he reached the place, old Spotted Calf was dead. He had torn the bandage entirely from the wound. There had been one red gush of blood, and the feeble old life went out on that small flood. Spotted Calf lay with his head against the rock.

Rusty wrapped the old body from head to foot in the robe. The pipe and the tobacco pouch troubled Rusty with desire, for he wanted a smoke badly. But after all one cannot rob the dead. Let poor Spotted Calf take with him to the Happy Hunting Grounds all the little possessions that he had brought to the Valley of Death.

Rusty re-crossed the valley. The three buzzards descended. Others dropped into view as though born out of nothingness. Rusty turned his back on them. Our graves must be of varying kinds, it seems.

That question that he had wanted to ask of Spotted Calf never would be answered now. Twice, in the raging, furnace-like heat of that day, Rusty drew out his knife and stared hungrily at the blade that could give him an answer of its own to all questions whatever. But still he had not struck the blow when the shadow swung out from the western cliff and slowly filled the valley with dimness, except for a ridge of fire at the top of the eastern wall.

His lips were so dry that they were cracking. His throat was as though he had swallowed dust.

He was feverish. Perhaps it was the fever, therefore, that made him seem to see something that stirred in the deep shadow of the western cliff just above the slanting talus of broken rock that sloped down toward the place where the body of Spotted Calf was now lying.

He looked again, curiously, with a start of fear. For what could it be that could issue out of solid rock? And then, on wide-spreading wings, a huge night owl came out of that shadow, a great, effortless, sailing disk of a bird that slid down across the valley straight toward Rusty Sabin.

And Rusty, with a wild cry, fell headlong down on the ground and heard the faint rush of the wings go over him.

When he could rise, he stared helplessly about him, but the great bird was gone.

There could be no doubt. It was the large bird from the Sacred Valley just beyond. It was that incarnation of Sweet Medicine that had learned to come to the hand of Rusty and take living food like a hawk stooping to a lure.

The soul of Rusty was too full for thought or speech. His knees shook under him. This was a sign indeed! This was a signal and a symbol from the Sky People and from their ruler, Sweet Medicine himself.

Rusty ran straight ahead. On his right he reached the base of the slanting heap of great boulders. Up the rocks he clambered, and, when he reached the top of the talus, he stared hungrily over the sheer face of the wall that rose above. There was nothing to be seen. There was only blankness, and one big, projecting ridge down the face of the rock.

Then why had Sweet Medicine flown from this place? Why, if not to give him a sign for liberation, had the god chosen to appear out of the solid wall of rock?

He clambered slowly across the top of the heaped boulders to the farther side of the projecting ridge.

There it stood before him, as tall, almost as wide as the entrance flap of a large teepee — a great, dark gash in the face of the cliff but so obscured by the ridge that it was invisible except from a single angle.

Rusty, without fear, with a wildly joyous laughter bubbling out of his throat, entered that darkness. With his hands he felt his way. Sometimes the passage narrowed so that he hardly could squeeze through. Sometimes it became low and he had to stoop, almost to crawl. Now it grew into a spacious room. Now it closed to a scant hallway. And at last he saw before him a red eye that widened, that grew, and finally he came out to the mouth of the cave that he had known before — the cave that overlooked the Sacred Valley and let him stare westward into the red of the sunset.

A trumpet beyond the power of human lips to sound blew through the Sacred Valley the next morning at sunrise and brought Rusty bounding to his feet from his bed of evergreen boughs. And his long, shrill, answering whistle raised a keen echo along the cliffs.

Afterward, he heard the faint beating of hoofs in a rapid rhythm, and finally up the valley, bursting like a silver bolt out of the clouds of trees, came White Horse, racing. He rushed around Rusty, flinging his heels, snorting, trampling down imaginary enemies, frantic with happiness, and Rusty laughed and laughed, with tears in his eyes.

After all, it was not strange. If the Indians blocked the way to the entrance to the Valley of Death, did not White Horse have brains at least as clever as those of a wild wolf?

Would he not think of returning to other places nearby where he had been with his master?

And yet Rusty did not take the thing as casually as this. All was mysterious from the moment when he carried the gold to the town of Witherell. With it, he had sought to give Richard Lester and his daughter all comfort. Instead, it had given Lester death. With it he had wished to fill the hands of the Cheyennes with gifts and bring honor on his friend, Standing Bull. But Standing Bull had almost died, might die now, in the meaningless hands of old Running Elk. And Rusty himself was driven out by white men and red alike.

Of all things under heaven, or above it, only one had remained true to him, and that was Sweet Medicine. Sweet Medicine, for purposes of his own, had sent him the signal and opened the door from the Valley of Death. Sweet Medicine had sent back, to be his comfort, the great shining white stallion.

And why had these things been done?

So that the life of Rusty Sabin could be devoted to the service of the god of the Indians. That much was, to Rusty, perfectly clear and simple. And, equally clear, in the gold of the Sacred Valley resided a curse. It was too terrible for men to handle.

That very first day he began his labor to cover the signs of his work when he had been delving for the treasure that white men so worship.

First, he constructed little traps along the runs that rabbits had made through the grass. All the other life in the Sacred Valley he would not touch, but rabbits, surely, had hardly a spirit to be protected. Sweet Medicine himself had proved that, evening after evening, when he flew down from his cave into the Sacred Valley and gripped a living prize out of the hand of Rusty.

When those traps were constructed and baited with the seed of grasses, Rusty fell to his important work even before he built for himself a shelter. He began to block the throat of the creek with big stones and fill the interstices with smaller stones and pebbles.

It was a great task, for the creek had cut for itself, at this narrow point, a little gorge fifteen feet deep. And since the work was to be lasting, Rusty used for it only the heaviest boulders that he could move with the strength of his hands and a strong pole for a lever to budge them. He worked for a week at this task, and many a device he used.

Even by the end of the first day he was weary enough. From the traps, before the twilight began, he took four fat rabbits and killed one for his own dinner, penned two in a little enclosure he had made when he was last in the Sacred Valley, and waited with the fourth rabbit in his arms, patiently, his face turned always toward the mouth of the cave, high up the cliff.

Now and then he chanted a brief phrase of prayer. And sometimes it seemed to him that the singing, deep voice of the waterfall gave him an answer, but the winged shadow did not appear.

Had he done wrong, therefore? Had he failed to please Sweet Medicine by his labors in the damming of the creek?

Anxiously he waited until the chill of the evening wind began to strike through him, and then, suddenly, the great winged shape was in the air.

It circled softly above him. He saw the talons, clearly, under the deeply feathered belly of the bird. He saw the cruel hook of the beak and the great, ominous, moon-like eyes. And he held up the poor rabbit by all four legs.

Down dropped the owl. The talons struck — marvelously missing the human fingers that held up this religious offering — and the rabbit screeched once like a child in agony. Afterward, it hung limply from the powerful claws and Sweet Medicine, in his guise as a bird, slid away over the treetops of the lower valley and was seen no more. From that moment, Rusty knew that all was well.

Chapter Nine

Charlie Galway succeeded in having Rusty driven out of the town, never to return unless to have his neck stretched by a hangman's rope, and it naturally occurred to Charlie that he was the heir, by right, to the entire life of Rusty. He himself, he said, would now become a trader and deal with the Indians.

His purpose was clear. Trading with the Indians would be the shield under which he would attempt to follow the back trail of Rusty, the back trail as far as the moment when Rusty Sabin had discovered the gold mine. It could not be that the gold that was found so readily, in such quantity, had been exhausted. Somewhere the mine must exist, and incredible wealth would go to the man who opened it again. The whole life of Charlie Galway might be devoted to this large purpose.

He felt that his way was open. It led back through the Cheyennes, of course, since it was while he was with the Indians that young Sabin had found the gold. Perhaps the Cheyennes would look upon Galway as an enemy? No, on the whole he was certain that he had appeared, on the night of the attempted lynching, rather as a friend than as an enemy. At least, that would be the interpretation Standing Bull was apt to put upon him.

But Rusty Sabin himself was dead. That report had come in across the plains with certainty.

It had been brought by a party of Pawnees who rejoiced with firewater and a great deal of noise over the death of the great scourge of their nation. The Cheyennes themselves, it was said, had penned Rusty up in the Valley of Death.

As for Standing Bull, he was a wreck, a mere gaunt skeleton who failed to return to vigorous manhood even though his wound had been healed. And the entire handling of that section of the tribe was left to the medicine man, Running Elk, who avoided war and showed himself a shrewd trader in the time of peace.

But there was a drought over the plains. The Indians were scattering far off toward the mountains in their effort to get plenty of water for their livestock. Even the inexhaustible water that flowed from the Sacred Valley of the Cheyennes, it was said, had been reduced to a mere dribble and threatened to fail altogether. It was under these circumstances, when a food shortage also was threatening, that Charlie Galway decided to undertake an excursion that should prove profitable in a small way and that should bring him, in some degree, close to the back trail of Rusty Sabin. In short, he would equip a small number of horses and mules with packs of food — corn and dried meat — add a certain amount of guns, powder and lead, and above all a good bit of whiskey. These goods he would exchange only for enough robes to pay the expenses of his journey. Then, to sweeten his reputation throughout the tribe, he would give away the rest of his merchandise, especially including the whiskey. He foresaw that he would become a most popular man with the Cheyennes, and certainly he would be in a position to ask all the questions he pleased about Rusty Sabin's past movements. And it would be a sad chance if he were not able to get swiftly and easily back onto the trail of the gold.

Since he had made himself the heir of Rusty's life, he did not see why he should not become the heir to Rusty's other and greatest possession — the love of young Maisry Lester.

Maisry, since the death of her father, had lived in an eager expectation of the return of Rusty, and, when the news came that Rusty was surely dead, a very odd transformation had occurred in her. The town of Witherell, which expected to see her pine away for a time at least, was amazed to see in her a sudden transformation.

She spent two days prostrated in grief, and on the third day she was seen at the market with a pale, calm, almost smiling face.

And this quiet calm of hers persisted.

If people spoke to her about Rusty, she looked either at the ground or at the far horizon and would not speak.

Some said that her poor brain was slightly addled by grief, but Charlie Galway was one who did not believe in a grief that extended over more than a few weeks, at the most. So he chose his time, and, when his merchandise was ready for the trip into the prairies, he went to see Maisry.

He found her in the cool of the back porch at a spinning wheel, singing a Cheyenne song.

She looked up without a start toward Charlie Galway and smiled a little as she bade him good day. He knew that he made a splendid figure. He had combed his long blond hair back across his shoulders; his broad hat had a great, crimson feather stuck into one side of it. His shirt and leggings were the purest, softest white of doeskin, worked as only Indian skill and patience could work it. The fringes were brightly beaded; the moccasins were delicately worked with beads, also. The rifle he leaned on gave a significance to his appearance, a purpose to his manhood.

"I didn't know that you were such a good hand with the Cheyenne language," he said.

"Rusty taught me," said the girl.

"Wasn't English good enough for him?" asked Galway.

"Why, you see he'd lived so long among the Cheyennes that English was only a thing to use when he asked for bread and butter, so to speak. He did his thinking in Cheyenne. He used to sing this song for me."

"It's a kind of a funny thing, ain't it?" said Galway. "I mean, for a man to be praying for sweet speech and light touching hands and soft falling feet."

"I suppose it is odd for a man to sing that song," said the girl. She looked away thoughtfully. "He wasn't like others."

"You're getting easier about him, ain't you?" said Charlie Galway. "What I heard was you wouldn't talk about him at all."

"I feel like talking about him today," said the girl.

"Why?" asked Galway.

"Well, I saw Colonel Miner ride by on his big gray horse. And it made me think about White Horse."

"White Horse sure has four legs under him," said Charlie. "But you know what I was thinking?"

"I don't know," said the girl.

"You can't go on grieving about Rusty all the days of your life, you know."

"I'm not grieving such a great deal," she said.

"No, I reckon everybody lets go, after a while, and gets nacheral again. What I mean is, you and me might be pretty friendly, Maisry."

"Of course we might," she answered.

"Yeah?" said Charlie. He came closer and leaned against a pillar of the porch. He said: "You see how I'm fixed up. I been doing pretty good in trading. Things are sort of coming my way. I'm going to be rich, one of these days. I'm going to be mighty rich." He gripped one hand into a fist and his eyes brightened.

"I think you are," she said, watching him. "I hope you are, too." She spun the wheel.

He reached out and stopped it. It made a soft hissing sound against the palm of his strong hand.

"You and me," he said, "why shouldn't we get married and team it together, Maisry?"

"Married?" she echoed. "Oh, no. I thought you were talking about friendship."

"I was. That's the best way to marry. You gotta marry sometime, don't you?"

"I don't know," she answered.

"I mean, you gotta have children, and all that."

She bent her head and looked down at her own breathing. "I couldn't have children unless Rusty were their father," she said.

"You couldn't? Why couldn't you?" he asked.

"I don't know. I can't marry, unless it's Rusty."

"You talk like you were a saint," said Charlie Galway.

"No, I'm not a saint," she replied. "Far from it."

"You're sure a funny one, though," said Charlie without scorn or anger. "You kind of beat me."

"I'm sorry."

"You got a kind of a blue nice kind of an eye," said Galway.

She looked straight at him so that he could study the blue of that eye as deliberately as he pleased.

"You know, Charlie," she said, "you ought not to fall in love with me. I don't think you will. But I'm simply warning you."

"You know something?" he answered, leaning well forward and staring. "I think I'm in love with you already."

"What makes you think so?"

"I never saw a knife or a rifle or a horse that I wanted as much as I want you, right now. That's love, ain't it?"

She shook her head.

"Go on and tell me, then," persisted Galway.

"When you love, you don't want to own a thing . . . you just want to join it."

"Come away from that. You can't tell me that," said Galway. "Why would a man love a woman if he didn't own her? Why would a woman love her children if she didn't own them?"

She considered this mystery for a time, and then shook her head again. "I can't put it into words," she said.

"Didn't Rusty act like he owned you?" asked Galway.

"No," she said thoughtfully. "I don't know how he acted. But not as though he owned me."

"Why, he would've made a squaw out of you!" cried Galway.

"I wish he had," said the girl. "But instead, he wanted to make a white man of himself, for my sake. And that was why he found the gold and brought it. And the gold has been the end of everything, and the death . . . the death . . ."

"Steady," said Galway.

"I'm sorry," murmured Maisry.

"Gee," said Galway, "but you are a most lovely-looking girl."

Chapter Ten

Charlie Galway started the next day for the distant Cheyennes. He chucked the thought of Maisry Lester over his shoulder as soon as he was outside the circle of the Witherell Hills. A long, hoarse hoot from the whistle of the river steamer was the last sound from civilization, and then he was out in the long, brown grass of the prairie. It was pale, sunburned, dry. It hurt the eyes with the strong reflection of the sun. It made the skin of his eyelids burn. A thin dust kept rising to his nostrils and made him cough a good deal the first day. Afterward, he settled to the work. He brought on his ten animals carefully. The second day, he missed one water hole, found a second crusted with cracking mud, and only by chance came on a bit of muddy water in the bottom of a draw. That water was what brought him through to the Cheyenne camp.

He was stopped when he was hardly in eyeshot of the white lodges and brought under guard into the village by a cluster of half a dozen young warriors. On the way, he talked with them, exercising his newly acquired Cheyenne, and they chattered back freely enough when they learned that he was a trader. For their food supply, they said, was running short in the village, and for a week not a drop of water had run past the mouth of the Sacred Valley, or at most small driblets that soon evaporated from the dry rocks of the gorge.

Disaster seemed to face the Cheyennes of this tribe. For that reason, all the more, the heart of Charlie Galway was light as he rode into the camp.

He was taken straight to the lodge of Standing Bull who, as the head chief, received all newcomers. And on a supple willow bed padded with buffalo robes, the sides of the lodge furled up to admit a free current of air, Charlie Galway saw a grim caricature of the copper giant who he had last looked at in Witherell,

The bones of Standing Bull were hardly covered by the dry, hard muscles. His ribs lifted out like gigantic fingers with every breath he drew. A pulse beat in the sunken hollow of his throat, but it throbbed with a feeble wavering. On the naked side of Standing Bull appeared, in dull purple, the round spot where the rifle bullet had driven into his body. That bullet had come from the gun of Galway, and Galway knew it, but there was no fear that the chief might recognize him and accuse him, even if he could have known what trigger finger had launched the bullet. For the starved face of Standing Bull turned continually to this side and to that, and his purple-gray lips were parted by mutterings that made only fragments of sense.

The eyes were worst — the shadow of them, and the red stain visible beneath the lids.

The man was dying, certainly, but slowly, and again the heart of Charlie Galway was lightened.

He went to the lodge of the medicine man next. In the teepee of Standing Bull he left merely a package of beads at which the sad-eyed squaws would hardly look. But at the home of Running Elk all was different.

An air of good cheer pervaded the teepee in spite of the unfortunate circumstances of the entire tribe. The squaws had a breezy air of conversation, and Running Elk himself deliberately admired with eye and hand the long strip of colored calico print that was unrolled. It was long enough to pass clear around the lodge, and it was a full yard in width. Running Elk crowed like a happy child when he saw the gaudy beauty of the pattern.

And in person he went out to supervise the trading. The goods were unpacked from the backs of the horses. Here again the guns and ammunition, the beads and the knives and hatchets were not considered very gravely, but the Indians brought out eagerly their best buffalo robes to trade for the corn and the dried beef.

There was still food in the village, but the supply of it was dwindling rapidly. For the lack of water, unless a rain fell soon or the supply from the Sacred Valley mysteriously was increased, they soon would have to begin to kill off their horses — and a tribe of Indians dismounted was like a tribe of wolves without legs to run on.

Before the loads of five horses had been disposed of, the trader had made twice the cost of the expedition. So he stood up and made a speech to this effect — that he was in his heart a brother to the Cheyennes, that he always had yearned to come among them and see some of their wisdom and hear some of their lore, and, therefore, he would not sell any more of his possessions to them. He would distribute freely. He would give to the lodges where only squaws lived, widows who were helpless in the tribe.

It was a rather moving speech, and, since it was followed straightway by the distribution of what was left of the goods, the words of Charlie Galway were looked on as the sheerest of truth. Afterward, a bearded white man dressed in all respects like one of the Cheyennes, put on a pair of spectacles and peered with earnestness into the face of the other.

"Come to my lodge and tell me what's in your mind, stranger," said the white Indian.

"What's your name, partner?" asked Galway.

"They call me Lazy Wolf. Will that suit you?"

"Anything you say," answered Galway, laughing, and went willingly with the trader.

As they passed on, Galway heard a chanting of women's voices, muffled by distance, and asked about it.

The trader answered: "That's a mean business. You take the Cheyennes most of the time and in most ways, and you'll find them a pretty upstanding people. But now and then the devil comes out of them . . . I mean, the devil of old customs. Those women yapping over there are getting ready to make a sacrifice of a living girl."

"Hold on," said Galway. "Living?"

"That's what I mean. They've got the habit of thinking that in a big pinch there's nothing so good as the sacrifice of a living person."

They entered the lodge of Lazy Wolf. It was larger than the other teepees, and instead of the white hides of buffalo cows, it was a double shell of the best canvas, the insulating air space between the two shells acting to shut out winter cold and summer heat. Even in the middle of this hot day the interior was only mildly warm.

As they sat down in the lodge, it seemed to Galway that he never before had seen furnishings so commodious in a tent. Besides the willow beds, there were backrests, and light, folding chairs; there was a rack for fishing tackle, another for rifles and revolvers, and over the fireplace leaned a little traveling crane on which several pots of varying sizes could be hung.

"When an Indian sees this outfit, doesn't your scalp fit a bit loose on your head?" asked Galway, staring enviously at the layout.

"I never know what I'll find in the lodge," said Lazy Wolf, grinning and stroking his short beard. "Whenever Blue Bird . . . that's my daughter . . . thinks that one of the braves or one of the squaws needs something, she gives it away if she can find it in my lodge."

"Gives it away?" echoed Galway, staring.

"That's the Indian in her," said Lazy Wolf.

"If she was a daughter of mine, I'd find a way of changing her habits," declared Galway with a stern conviction.

"Maybe you would," answered the trader. "But these are bad days for her. When an Indian is sad, she always starts giving things away. Love is a devilish thing, Galway."

"Oh . . . love, eh?" said Galway with a shrug of his shoulders.

"Never bothered you much?" asked Lazy Wolf.

"Not a lot," said Galway.

"It may hit you later on," said Lazy Wolf. "The Cheyenne girl I married died when Blue Bird was born. I've tried to go back and live among my own people . . . but I miss something when I'm away. Love is a queer thing, Galway, but you're too young to know about it, perhaps."

"Aye, maybe," said Galway. "Won't the chief she's in love with have anything to do with her?"

"It's a dead man," said Lazy Wolf. "It's Red Hawk that I'm talking about."

"Ah, you mean Rusty Sabin?"

"Did you know him?"

"A little . . . yes."

"Not enough to be his friend?"

"I'd call myself his friend," said Galway.

Lazy Wolf rubbed his beard into a staring confusion. He pondered, and then delivered his conclusion: "Different from other people. There was no way of marking where the Indian stopped in him and the white man began. He was more credulous than a Cheyenne about a good many things, and keener than any white man about others. He hated pain, but he loved battle. If you showed him a thing hard to do, he couldn't help wanting to do it. He saw White Horse . . . and no other horse existed for him afterward. Nothing in the world existed for him. He spent a year chasing that horse. And he caught it . . . on foot . . . and he caught it."

"That sounds kind of impossible," said Galway.

"A man with a heart like Rusty Sabin's . . . why, you can't measure what the man can do unless you can measure the heart. There was no measuring of the heart of Rusty Sabin. No man could tell what a friend he was. It was for a friend that he died. It was for a friend that he was driven out by the whites. The

Cheyennes murdered him. But he didn't fight against it because he believed in the religious ceremony . . . he thought it was the right way of bringing health back to Standing Bull. But there's one thing he would have prevented, if he had been here today, and that is the sacrifice of a living girl to end the drought."

"Could he have stopped them?" asked Galway curiously.

"He would have found a way," said the trader. "I don't know how. He always found a way to do what he wanted in a pinch. Ah, here they come now."

The chanting of the women came toward them out of the distance with an accompaniment of blowing horns. It was not music. It was not even melodious noise. To Galway it breathed out a savage fury.

"You mean that they simply pick out a girl and then murder her?" asked Galway.

"They don't pick her out. There's always some girl that's willing to make the sacrifice for the sake of the tribe. Then they take her to the Valley of Death . . . a big box cañon that even a bird could hardly fly out of. And the girl will walk in freely. She won't have to be dragged. Afterward, part of the Cheyennes will keep guard over the mouth of the Valley of Death and the other half will go to the entrance to the Sacred Valley, and pray to Sweet Medicine to send them water to end the drought."

"It's a queer idea," said Galway. "What's in the Sacred Valley?"

"I don't know," said the trader. "No living man ever has been inside it and came out to tell what was there. An Indian would rather step into a bonfire than into the Sacred Valley."

"No one ever went inside?" demanded Galway again.

"Don't try it yourself," said Lazy Wolf. "If the Indians saw you try it, they'd knife you. If they ever heard that you'd gone inside, they'd trail you to the end of the world and get your scalp to make a sacrifice to Sweet Medicine."

It's as bad as all that, is it?" asked Galway, setting his fighting chin. "And no one ever dared to go inside?"

"No one. That is, excepting Rusty Sabin."

"Ah?" cried Galway. An idea had taken fire in his mind. "He went in? Rusty Sabin went in . . . and the Indians didn't know about it?"

"They knew about it, but it was different with Rusty. He was a sort of chosen spirit . . . a sacred man . . . chosen by Sweet Medicine, I mean. And he brought back to the tribe the sacred arrow, which is the most holy thing they possess today. He saw Sweet Medicine in the form of a huge owl."

"The devil he did. You say this as though you believed it."

"It isn't a question of what I believe," said Lazy Wolf. "It's merely that Rusty believed it. And that was enough for me. That was enough for the Cheyennes, too."

"This here Rusty was a sort of a prophet or something, eh?" asked Galway.

"You can call him that. He was almost that," said the trader. "I've never known a man like him. I'll never find another fit to step in his shoes."

The noise of the procession began to roar in front of the lodge.

"Let's have a look at this," said Galway, and pushed open the entrance flap of the teepee.

He saw before him at the head of the rout old Running Elk himself, almost naked, streaked and flaming with paints of all colors, and with a buffalo's head on his shoulders. He danced with wild boundings; he screeched weird words and phrases that the rout behind him echoed.

There came, first of all, a dozen braves on horseback with their spears reversed, their faces blackened. Behind them, on a beautiful little black pony, rode a girl crowned with flowers and shining in the finest of soft, white doeskin dresses. Her horse was led by two warriors. She herself sat on the saddle with uplifted face, smiling, her hands folded in her lap. And it seemed to the startled eyes of Galway that not even the blue and golden beauty of Maisry Lester approached the loveliness of the Cheyenne. She was not the dark copper but much lighter; there was only enough stain in her skin to give it a luminous richness. And she was the sacrifice. Galway knew that. He caught his breath at the thought of such a creature going willingly to death,

Then Lazy Wolf rushed violently past him shouting: "Blue Bird! Blue Bird!"

The girl rode on as though she had not heard. Several of the warriors who followed the sacrifice turned and put the points of their spears at the breast of the trader. He fell on his knees and began to beat his fists against his face.

Chapter Eleven

The beating of drums, the blowing of horns, and the chanting of voices poured into the Sacred Valley, so that the antelope flashed their white disks of warning and fled up toward the peaceful waters of the lake. The huge buffalo lifted their heads to listen and let the dry grass drip down from their mouths, unchewed; the elk made their proud stand, and one of the grizzlies, as Rusty Sabin watched, stood up with his vast paws folded on his breast in an attitude very like that of prayer.

Rusty whistled. White Horse gleamed through the brush and came dazzling out into the sunset light. He had to make a frisking turn or two before Rusty could leap onto his back, and then at a dizzy gallop, like water shooting down a long flume, they swept through the Sacred Valley, over the dry meadows deep in standing pasture, through the grooves, and beside the lower pools of standing water. For the river no longer ran, and the chanting of the waterfall was silent in the valley. Only a small trickle darkened the face of the cliff where the waterfall usually fell in a white thunder.

Near the foot of the Sacred Valley, Rusty dismounted and stood at the head of the narrow entrance gorge. The big trees arose on one side. On the other, the cavernous wall of the ravine rose in successive hollows above him.

He could hear a tumultuous uproar of instruments and chanting. And this having died down to a murmur, he recognized the voice of Running Elk, chanting to Sweet Medicine a solo that was the old Cheyenne prayer for rain.

He had an impulse to rush out among them. He was overcome with a vast desire to see their faces. The human sound of the voices, the familiar words of the prayer brought tears to his eyes. He was young, and he had been long alone.

But he turned and went back to the place where White Horse was waiting. On the back of the stallion he returned moodily to the upper end of the valley and looked up toward the mouth of the cave of Sweet Medicine.

Would the god appear to make an answer to his worshippers? Or was Sweet Medicine hovering, now, over the Valley of Death?

He dismounted from the horse. It was the end of the day. Only a dim greenness remained around the horizon, where a big, boat-shaped moon was floating upward.

There was no sign at the mouth of the cave. And suddenly Rusty knew that he would have to look into the Valley of Death. He lifted his hands, palm upward, and prayed silently to the god. Then he climbed the face of the rock, where he had cut, with much labor, the rough flight of steps all the way to the lip of the cave. When he reached the place, he peered earnestly into the darkness of the hollow cavern; his knees were weak and trembling.

Then he entered the cave, saying in a voice that wavered with fear: "It's I. It is Red Hawk. It is your servant. Be merciful, Sweet Medicine."

So he went on through the thick darkness, breathing hard, feeling his way. Once he thought that a whisper ran past him, and his blood turned to ice. But at last he came to the other end of the passage and looked down into the moonlit valley. Over it hovered dim shapes, the buzzards waiting on the wing for their prey. And in the white hollow of the cañon he saw the Indian girl, a tiny shape kneeling with hands lifted. The heart of Rusty Sabin swelled; a great stroke of blood rushed through his brain. And he swore that it was the voice of the god speaking inside him.

Therefore he climbed down the great slope of broken rocks to the floor of the ravine. Once he was there, the old shudder of horror came over him. He felt minutely small as he looked up to the towering lift of the cliffs. So it was when mere mortality measured itself against the gods. He had to stop and pray again, looking back toward that place on the western cliff from which he had seen the god issue in his usual guise, as a night owl. But there was no sign except that stroke of hot blood through his brain.

He went on again, keeping some of the big boulders between himself and the girl, until he could hear her voice, still praying: "This life which I give away to you, Sweet Medicine, is not a great gift. It is no more to you than a single bead on a moccasin is to me. Perhaps you do not want unhappy souls in your heaven. But if you will have me, I go gladly. Give me a sign, if it is your will to accept me. . . ."

Rusty, drawn by the words, stepped suddenly from the side of the rock.

The girl, starting up from her knees, screamed. The scream stopped as though a hand had throttled it. Blue Bird fell in an odd little heap of shining white doeskin.

"She is dead," said Rusty, staring down at her. "The god has taken her."

He was afraid to touch her. He kneeled beside the motionless body. If he laid hand on her, perhaps the god would strike him, also, and was he ready to die?

At last, steeling himself, he touched her cheek with tentative fingers. It was strangely warm. But death, after all, had not had time to turn her cold. He laid his hand over her heart. Through the supple softness of the deerskin he surely could feel the slight stirring of the pulse, but he could not distinguish the throbbing.

She was dead, then, and this was the way Sweet Medicine accepted the chosen souls that were offered as a sacrifice.

He lifted her and her head and arms and legs fell loosely down. He had to make a cradle of his arms to support her limp weight, with her head against his shoulder.

A thin shadow streaked over him. He heard the small whisper of wings and, looking up, saw the moon strained through the wing feathers of a buzzard.

Since the god had accepted her it was not right that she should be harried by the things of evil and go mangled to the other world. Sweet Medicine should see her as she was among the Cheyennes. The god should see the long, delicate curling of the eyelashes. He should touch this softness of flesh. Even on the blue fields of heaven the Sky People never could have seen a miracle more wonderful than the curving beauty of her lips.

Then he realized that it was for this special mission that he had been drawn, at the will of the god, out of the Sacred Valley and into the Valley of Death. It was because Sweet Medicine wished to have her borne up to his own dwelling in the rock.

He bore her to the bottom of the slope of rocks. There he rested a moment. For one made so slenderly, so light-footed, she was surprisingly heavy, he thought. Now he was climbing over the boulders, panting, straining, until he reached the top and the hidden entrance to the cave.

He had to pause there. Looking down earnestly into the face of the girl, he moved into the cave and saw the steep shadow slide over her face. It was the last he would see of her. He stood for a moment with that thought, and then went on into the tunnel. It was not easy to get her through some of the narrow and low places, but at last he came to the largest part, near the entrance on the side of the Sacred Valley. Here he kneeled and laid the body on the floor. In the darkness he found her hands and crossed them on her breast. He smoothed her hair. He put her feet together and drew down the velvet softness of the doeskin skirt. When the god, whose immortal eyes do not need the light of day, should look on her for the first time, he would cry out with astonishment at her beauty. He would cover his open mouth with his hand. And then Sweet Medicine would laugh with pleasure.

He said: "Sweet Medicine, I lift my hands to you. I have brought the sacrifice to the floor of your lodging. I hope to hear you laugh with joy when you see her. But remember, god that you are, that she is young and she is only a woman. If you come to her in the likeness of an owl with great burning eyes and a hooked beak, fear might kill her spirit a second time. Come to her as you were in the years long ago, when you walked the earth as a man, with your lance in your hand, and the wind in your hair, and the green springtime following you over the prairies."

A murmur whispered beneath him: "Red Hawk . . ."

"It is I!" exclaimed Rusty. "Blue Bird. Where are you? How far away are you? Where is your spirit walking? Can you see me from heaven?"

"Am I dead?" said the girl.

"Yes, yes!" cried Rusty. "You are dead. Only your voice has been put into your throat for a moment to give me a last message. Do you find yourself in the high blue of the Happy Hunting Grounds?

"I seem to be in thick darkness," she murmured. "It's as though I had been falling. . . ."

"Is the god sending you back to earth?" cried Rusty.

"I don't know. I thought I was in the Valley of Death, and then I saw you . . . and I knew that you were a ghost. Where are we?"

"We are on the earth, in the house of Sweet Medicine. Have no fear. Has your spirit really returned to you? Does the god wish you to live again?" He laid his hand over her heart. Unquestionably there was a steady pulsation.

"Blue Bird, we both are living!" shouted Rusty suddenly. "Sweet Medicine took you away and gave you back again when I prayed to him . . . . Shall I carry you, or can you stand . . . . So? Walk close to me. Keep one hand out to ward off the wall of the cave. There . . . you can see the moonlight ahead of us. . . ."

"How can you be flesh and warm blood?" asked the girl. "They carried you to the Valley of Death."

"When the god wills it, what is life or death?" asked Rusty, laughing with joy. "He takes and he gives again. He made me go to you . . . he made me carry you to his house . . . and there he breathed on you while I prayed. I heard a whisper go by me. It was the unseen god. He touched you when I could not see. He laid his finger on your lips, and you began to breathe. He touched your heart and it beat once more. And he gave me happiness. Do you feel it also?"

"If this were the blue path across the sky and we were walking it together, I could not be happier," said the girl.

Now they stood at the mouth of the cave.

"Do you see?" he asked her.

"What is it? I never have seen such a valley."

"Hush. This is the Sacred Valley."

She uttered a cry and caught up her hands across her eyes. "Shall I die because I have seen it?" she asked.

"You will live because you have seen it. It is Sweet Medicine who has brought you here. This is his will and pleasure. Look again."

She slowly drew down her hands from her eyes.

"How is it with you now?"

"My eyes drink in happiness. My soul tastes it," she said. "All the prairies are burned and dry, but see how much water Sweet Medicine keeps here in his hand. Will he pour it out upon the Cheyennes before they die of thirst, and before they have killed all their horses?"

"He will save his people," said Rusty confidently. "And I think that I see how he will do it. Come down with me. Be careful. The steps in the rock are not cut very deep. And yet if you fell, I think that the god would spread his wings under you. Your spirit is fresh from heaven . . . that is why I feel such a delight to be with you."

Chapter Twelve

They stood by the lake. The water was still. The moon path lay broad and bright before them and the stars looked up from either side.

"Red Hawk, I am not dead?" whispered the girl. "This must be heaven, and you are no ghost beside me."

"Ghosts have no shadows," he told her. "And see our reflections at our feet."

"Is that whispering the wind in the trees?"

"It may also be the god," said Rusty. "I don't know, except that, when he passes, I feel the wind blow through my spirit."

"And you are not afraid?"

"He is a father and protects me."

"Will he never appear before you?"

"Yes, in the early morning or the evening, or often on a moonlit night like this. He comes as a great, wide-winged owl."

"*Ai! Ai!* Do not call him. I am afraid."

"There is nothing to fear. He loves me. He will keep harm far away from everything that is dear to me."

"Ah . . . do you say that with your heart or with your lips only?"

"I say it from my heart, of course. Look."

A huge buffalo bull came from among the trees, waded into the lake, belly deep, and drank. He was not seven steps away from them.

"Shall we run?" the girl said breathlessly.

But he answered in a calm voice that was not lowered: "There is no reason to be afraid. The buffalo are the wise souls of dead warriors who Sweet Medicine loved. He brought them here and gave them happiness in the Sacred Valley."

The big bull, lifting his head, turned it slowly toward them. Water streamed in dribblings from his muzzle. His eyes were two dangerous little points of brightness under the shag of hair on his brow. He blew out a great breath and darkened the water with the wind of his breathing.

"Ah, how beautiful," said the girl, still whispering. "See how silken fat his flanks are. And his horns are polished . . . they are waxed and polished more than war bows."

"If you whisper, the soul of the dead man will be angry," said Rusty. "I think he is angry now . . . *ha!* . . . you see that whispering is bad manners when there are the spirits of the brave near us."

The bull, lurching suddenly out of the water, turned toward the two with lowered head. He stamped the ground till it shook under the hoof and he rolled his big, blunt horns threateningly to one side.

"Run . . . he will charge!" cried the girl.

Rusty lifted his right hand in the signal of greeting.

"Oh, brother," he said, "forgive her for foolishness. It is very hard for a woman to be wise. Silly little things keeping blowing into their minds like bright autumn leaves on the wind. But this one is a chosen spirit. She has been to the heaven of Sweet Medicine. See! She is now alive and standing in the Sacred Valley."

The buffalo turned with a final sway of the head and strode away into the brush. His hoof falls died out.

"If that was the soul of a warrior, he must have been a great chief," said the girl. "How could you endure to stand so close? What if he had struck his horns into your body because he was angry about my foolish whispering?"

"That would have been the will of Sweet Medicine, and there's no use trying to avoid what the god determines.

"I'm almost afraid of you, when you talk like that."

"You should not be. Do you hear, far, far away, the horns blowing and the moan of the people, praying for rain? They have been there since the sunset. My poor countrymen."

"Do you pity?"

"My heart aches for them."

"But they drove you out to the Valley of Death."

"That was the malice of Running Elk and the simplicity of the braves who could believe him. But in all of that, they were working the will of Sweet Medicine. He wished to bring me back to the Sacred Valley."

"How did he take you from the Valley of Death to the Sacred Valley?"

"I was ready to die, and then I saw Sweet Medicine in the form of the great owl fly out of the cliff across the valley. His spirit led me through the rock as I led you."

"Ah, how wonderful. My heart turns cold when you talk like this. To live as you do with a god in every day of your life must be a glorious thing."

"You're trembling," he said.

"The wind is a little chilly," she said.

"Sit closer to me. Are you warmer now?"

"Ah, yes."

"Are you happy?"

"Yes."

"Do you know how it is with me? Joy keeps flashing up through my heart like swift trout out of shadow into golden sunshine. Is it so with you?"

"Yes."

"Then should we be married?"

"Yes."

"There are no people here to make the ceremony," he said.

"Well, if you lift me in your arms and carry me over the threshold of your lodge, that would be a marriage, in the Sacred Valley."

"Is it true?" he asked with his head lifted. "Sweet Medicine, give me an answer. Come swiftly into the valley and give me an answer."

He waited through a long moment. The sky remained empty, filled only with the moonlight as with a shining mist. The girl, as he watched, had lifted her hand as though to ward off an impending stroke.

"There is no sign," he said slowly.

"Look back at me," pleaded the girl. "Is it really Sweet Medicine about whom you're thinking? Or are you remembering the white girl?"

"Yes. I think of her, also."

"She is the one you care about. I never would be the real wife. I would only be the squaw for using the flesh-scraper on the hides, and cutting wood, and carrying water. She would sit in the lodging and bead the moccasins, and comb your hair, and sit with your head in her lap, laughing at the poor slave, Blue Bird, that went drudging back and forth."

He said nothing. She began to weep. She doubled up her hands into fists. Her weeping did no more than give pauses to her torrent of speech.

"I am only a worthless thing because I have red skin. She is white and golden and blue. She belongs to your own people."

"The Cheyennes are my own people," he said. "Now I would like to comfort you, because you talk like an angry child. But there is a little truth in what you say. I do think, still, of Maisry Lester. But she belongs to a life to which I can never return. She is parted from me. I never shall see her again."

"Do you mean that?" asked Blue Bird hungrily.

"Yes, I mean it. She would not be my wife, if I had another. White men only may marry once."

"If a great chief had only one wife, then he never would have many comforts in his teepee."

"That may be true," he said. "But, also, if she came into the Sacred Valley, it would not be sacred to her. Sweet Medicine would be no more than a night owl. For the whites have no belief in anything. However, she never would sit and cry like a child."

"I'm sorry. Forgive me. And I think that if Sweet Medicine sent me to you all the way from heaven, as you say, then you should take me."

"I never wanted anything so much. *Ah hai*, the tears of a woman come and go and have no meaning. Your lips are still trembling, but now you commence to laugh. Why are you laughing at me?"

"Because the god has poured into me such happiness that it overflows. *Ai, ai, ai!* I could cry out to the moon. I could sweep the stars out of the sky and weave them into a chain like flowers. The moonlight shines through me. If the god looks down now from the sky, he sees me shining like the face of his lake. Sweet Medicine, do not let evil come because I sit here laughing, while my people are mourning and begging you to send the rain. Sweet Medicine, be merciful. Red Hawk, will the god be angry with me?"

"I don't think so. This moment you are so delightful that the Sky People must be starting out of their sleep and find that they are dreaming of the earth dwellers. They must be looking down into the Sacred Valley and beginning to smile. Let the morning come quickly, and then Sweet Medicine will give us the answer."

"What answer?"

"He will say whether he wants you to stay here with me or to go away."

"Ah, will he speak to you with words?"

"He will take the food from your hand as he does from mine when he is pleased. But if he avoids you, then you must go away."

"Tell me another thing."

"Yes. Whatever you please."

"Tell me the best words to use in order to pray to the god."

Chapter Thirteen

All night through, the chanters maintained the prayer to the god. But by turns, the groups of warriors danced in the moonlight, or chanted, or beat on the drums, or drew howling noises from the horns.

Still, when the moon died in the east before the growing light of the sun, there was not a sign of answer from the careless god. There was not a shadow of a cloud on the horizon, and another summer day was promised, as brazen hot as the ones that had scorched the prairies before. Still, when the braves looked toward Running Elk for a permission to stop the entreaties, the long-faced old man would make no sign.

And inside the valley, far up toward the holier end, beside the shining edge of the lake and opposite the cave of Sweet Medicine, Blue Bird stood up with a living rabbit grasped in her strong young hands. Behind her, Red Hawk whistled a long, shrill note, and now the miracle happened, drawing a cry of fear from the lips of the girl. For she saw, on the lip of the cave above her, a huge owl, greater than any eye ever had beheld before. It extended its wings. It rushed down through the air toward her. She heard the thin whispering of those furred wing feathers. She saw the great hooked talon drawn up toward the soft feathers of the belly. She saw the round shining of the eyes. So a god would take food from her hand and bless her.

But in the last moment the owl swerved. Its talons reached out and the powerful legs behind them as though of their own volition they still would have seized on the rabbit. But the wings slid the great bird rapidly away.

The cry of the girl slashed through the brain of Red Hawk. She fell on her knees and let the rabbit go bounding away, its ears flattened by the speed of its running. And so, her arms thrown up, the girl cried out after the owl.

But the bird, veering without a wing flap, swerved suddenly back toward the cave and disappeared into the mouth of it.

Red Hawk picked up from the ground a little fluffy owl feather that had fluttered down close to Blue Bird. He put it in her hair, sadly.

"You must go," he said. "You see that the god is not angry if you do as he wishes at once. He has given you a token of his favor. Take it. Let that make you happy. Perhaps on some other day you may come back into the Sacred Valley and live here forever. Or is his anger with me, also? We shall see."

He picked up another rabbit, its four feet tied securely together, and once more he whistled. And again the mighty owl dipped off the edge of the cliff and slid through the air with faultless ease. Right down he came, struck the talons of one foot into the offered rabbit, and veered away again to disappear inside the cave.

The girl began to beat her face with her hands and cry out: "He will not accept me! He turns his face from me! I want to die! I don't want to live!"

"Think how the Cheyennes will admire you and wonder at you," said Red Hawk. "No other Indian ever has been inside the Sacred Valley and gone out alive again. You went in at the Valley of Death . . . you will come out from the Sacred Valley with the token of the god worn in your hair. Why, Blue Bird, you will become at once almost greater medicine than Running Elk."

"But I shall be alone," said the girl. "I'd rather die here in the valley than live in any other place."

"There is the will of the god to think about," he told her. "He sent you back from death into life. Now he is sending you back to the Cheyennes. Will you stop and argue with him?"

Afterward, he caught trout and roasted them over the coals of a quick fire. He wrapped the fish in broad leaves, and, when the leaves were seared and rotten with the flame, he took out the fish. They were so tender that he could lift out the frame of bones. It was a delicacy.

Blue Bird, as she ate, fell into a happy dream. There was so much to see that she could not turn her head everywhere. It was all sacred. The cliffs, the trees, the grass, all was different from the beings in the outer world. And the animals moved with more beauty, more peaceful dignity than any others she had seen.

He took Blue Bird into the house he had built. She was overcome with wonder, and, when he tried to explain how he had done each part of the work, she merely shook her head.

"Ah, yes . . . with your own hands, but with Sweet Medicine standing invisible beside you. Sweet Medicine lifted the stones of the dam, also. You could not have done it without him."

"Perhaps not," he agreed.

* * * * *

It was time for her to go. The sun was up. Wheeling flights of birds rose out of the trees and flew down the valley.

"They are pointing you the way you must take," he said.

She had grown composed.

"My grandmother told me," she said, "that men are made for hunting and battle and glory, but women are meant for pain. *Ai, ai!* I have breathed in such pain, when I think of leaving the valley, that my heart is swollen and great with it. Only tell me this . . . shall I see you again before I die?"

He touched the owl feather in her hair. "This is the proof that you belong to Sweet Medicine," he said. "Therefore I surely shall see you again."

He called White Horse and helped the girl onto the back of the stallion. The rustling of her white dress maddened him. White Horse danced and curvetted, ready to fling her to the ground.

She clung to the windy mane. And the voice of Red Hawk was half stopped with happy laughter as he controlled the great horse with words, for he thought that he never before had seen a picture so beautiful as the golden loveliness of the girl mounted on the silken white flashing of the stallion.

So they went down the valley, side-by-side, White Horse growing quieter. At the mouth of the entrance ravine they halted and she slipped to the ground.

He said: "When you go among the people, tell them to continue their chanting, because Sweet Medicine will send them water. He has told me what to do to answer their prayers. Tell the people that you have seen the god and that he has given you the feather as a token that you belong to him . . . he has accepted you. But if you speak of anything else that you saw in the Sacred Valley, you surely will die."

She stepped close to him until her forehead leaned against his shoulder. He listened to her breathing in a pause of the weary chanting that still sounded beyond the entrance rocks.

"Are you a little unhappy because I have to go?" she asked.

"I am so sad," he said, "that my throat aches." He lifted one hand to the sky. "Sweet Medicine," he said, "go with her . . . bring her happiness . . . lead her again to me or me to her. Fill my mind and my hands with many things to do so that my heart shall not be empty when I remember her."

"Is there a token? Is there an answer?" she asked.

He said: "The wind bends the feather in your hair toward me. It is the answer. My prayer shall be granted."

She looked at him for a moment with a shining face. Afterward, her head lifted, she went slowly down the narrow of the gorge.

Red Hawk went back up the valley on the back of the stallion.

He began to roll from the places the big rocks with which he had built the wall of the dam.

Chapter Fourteen

Withdrawn from the Cheyennes who danced and sang and beat the drums in front of the Sacred Valley, Galway watched the ceremonies with an unceasing interest. He was learning more and more of these people. And the more he learned, the more his heart burned with eagerness to pass through the forbidden gate of the valley.

Through the early morning, as the sun rose, he saw the trader, Lazy Wolf, come on the back of a brown mule. The bowed head and shoulders of the man told of the misery that weighed him down. He sat the mule for a moment, staring at the chanting Indians. Then he came to Galway and dismounted.

"No luck?" asked Galway, with a touch of sympathy.

"I offered the Cheyennes who are guarding the entrance of the Valley of Death the value of a hundred horses. That's as high as they can count. But that wouldn't shake them. They keep the valley closed. I went to the mouth of it and shouted with all my might. But I never got an answer. I suppose she's dead even by this time."

"I'm sorry for it," said Galway.

"I'll leave the tribe," said the trader. "God knows that life among the whites will be an empty thing for me, but I can't stay among these people and think of murder every time I see their faces."

Here there was a sudden cessation of the chanting, a wild outbreaking of many voices that shouted: "Blue Bird! Blue Bird!"

Only Running Elk, on his tireless old legs, kept jogging around and around the circle, mumbling the formula of the chant, the prayer for "Rain, rain, rain!" By his persistence all the efforts that had gone into this great praying would not be broken and wasted. But his eyes rolled wildly in his head and his dancing faltered and almost stopped.

For Blue Bird, Galway saw, was walking calmly out of the mouth of the Sacred Valley, past the huge columns of the cliffs that guarded the ravine. She came with her head high, smiling a little, and an air of strange dignity made her seem older.

Lazy Wolf, shouting out in a sudden frenzy, rushed toward her.

A dozen strong hands caught and held him fast.

"She has come through the Sacred Valley . . . purify yourself before you touch her!" they cried to him.

Others were heaping dry sweet grass on the fire so that they could wash themselves in the smoke that rose in a cloud. And the rest, prancing back to keep at a safe distance from this girl who should have been a lifeless ghost, surrounded her with their gestures of wonder.

She paid no attention to Lazy Wolf at first. She stood in the center of the beaten ground where the dancing had been continuing and raised a hand that silenced even the mumbling chant of Running Elk. He sank exhausted to one knee and listened, as the girl said: "I have seen the god. He has heard the prayers of the Cheyennes. He will send you water. Sing to him. Praise him. He will send you water at once."

The uproar deafened Galway. Every Indian was roaring like a bull. They were dancing, flinging up their arms. And Lazy Wolf at last had the girl in his embrace.

Galway made his way to them. He could hardly hear the words of the girl, he was so obsessed in staring at her. For she was transformed. There was a calmness and a removal of interest from the ordinary world of ordinary men. In her dignity there was sadness, also. A strange little chill of superstition and fear ran quickly through the blood of Galway.

She was saying: "If I speak of what I saw in the Sacred Valley or what appeared to me in the Valley of Death, I should die. I cannot tell you what comes to the souls of brave men and good women when they die. I cannot tell you what happiness comes to them. I can only show you the symbol of Sweet Medicine. I saw him. He drew the life from my body, and then breathed it back into my nostrils. He stopped my heart and made it beat again. He bore me into the blue of the Happy Hunting Grounds, and then he returned me to the earth to show the Cheyennes that he loves them, they are his people."

They came slowly about her, their hands stretched out. One by one they touched the flare of her skirt or the deerskin shirt, or the hair that flowed down her back. But not one of them dared to touch the little owl feather when she pointed to it.

Some of the dread passed out of Galway when he saw that feather.

He said to the trader, whose eyes were bright with tears of happiness: "Your girl knows how to tell a good yarn while she's about it."

"People see what they believe in," said Lazy Wolf. "She wouldn't lie. She'd cut her tongue out sooner than lie. And if you suggest to one of these Cheyennes that perhaps she's lying about what's happened to her, you'll have a knife in your throat before you finish talking."

"Why the devil should that be?" asked Galway,

"Because now she's an honor and a glory to the tribe. You see? Every Cheyenne is a bigger and a better man because one of their people went through the Sacred Valley and lived to come among them again."

Galway, narrowing his eyes, listened and nodded.

Then, out of the distance, an obscure roaring noise began, rolled toward them, grew greater, thundered in the very throat of the entrance ravine.

What Galway saw, first of all, was a cloudy white head of spray, like a mist driving on a storm wind. And afterward a tumultuous head of water sluiced out into the empty cañon, brimmed it with thunder, sent up waving flags of spray into the morning sunlight.

The Cheyennes fell flat on the ground in the face of the miracle; Galway himself felt his knees shaking. His heart was in his throat, choking him.

He knew the strange stories of the Indian superstitions and of mysterious rainmakers who had brought rain after long drought by incantations. But this was a miracle of another sort. This was a different matter, for by a veritable act of heaven a torrent had been made to spring out in the midst of a dry land.

He was baffled. His brain stubbornly refused to accept the facts that he had seen. He was a gloomy face and figure as he traveled back with the Cheyennes toward their camp.

The whole aspect of creation was changed for them now. Every pool and standing backwater of the ravine was filled with sweet, fresh water. There was ample to drink for their livestock for ten days to come. And since Sweet Medicine had sent them this quick sign of his favor, surely he would not fail to send them the rain, also. So they sang and laughed and shouted cheerfully to one another.

Hardly had they reached the Cheyenne encampment before other news came to them. The water-famished buffalo had found the smell of water on the wind and were beginning to troop in thousands to the drinking holes in the bed of the river. Already the hunters were out and bringing back skins and horse loads of the meat. It was like one of the great spring huntings, after a starving winter. The back of the famine was broken!

Very greatly the Cheyennes were honoring their god. What had the white men, what had the Pawnee wolves or the Sioux to show in comparison with Sweet Medicine? The encampment was filled with dancing and howling songs, and even the dogs grew excited and ran, yelping in noisy crowds.

Blue Bird, entering the village, was received as never a woman before had been welcomed. Two famous warriors, on foot, led her horse by the bridle. And the whole population of the tribe flocked around her with raised hands.

The warriors led her horse on slowly since they knew that the people would not be satisfied until every one of them had managed to touch the garments of this new prophetess. And she accepted this homage with a sad and resigned dignity rather than with a girlish joy.

Therefore even the women were not very jealous of her new honors. They muttered to one another: "It is plain that she has seen the god. I won't need to see the owl feather in her hair. It's enough to see her face. She will never be happy again, poor Blue Bird. She has seen too much of heaven ever to be contented with the earth again."

She asked to be taken to the lodge of Standing Bull, and therefore that was her first stopping place.

The fever had left him for the moment; he lay with sunken eyes, a dreadful skeleton. His lips had shrunk against the teeth. He seemed an old man.

He said to Blue Bird: "They have told me. I know that a good woman can go farther toward the Sky People than the bravest man. But have you a message for me, Blue Bird?"

She sat down on her heels beside him and laid her hand on his forehead. "Do you feel something come over you from the touch of my hand?" she asked.

"A sort of coolness and a peace," said Standing Bull.

"It is the blessing of Sweet Medicine," said the girl.

"*Ah hai!* It is the word from the god?" breathed the war chief.

"You are to be cured."

Standing Bull closed his eyes and groaned.

"But Sweet Medicine wishes that you should taste no food except what I prepare for you."

"Willingly. But that is not possible. Running Elk gives me every day a new potion. I must take that or he will be angry."

"Let me have the drink," said the girl.

One of the squaws brought a bowl and gave it with a trembling hand to this visitor from the sky. Blue Bird tasted a foul and bitter mixture that made her head sing at once.

"Do you fear Running Elk more than you fear Sweet Medicine?" she asked.

"No, no, no," muttered Standing Bull.

Blue Bird flung the contents of the bowl into the fire. The squaws cried out with shrill voices. One of them ran in wild haste out of the lodge. Standing Bull himself gathered his strength to lift himself on one elbow and watch the cloud of steam and smoke and dust of ashes that fountained up into the air as high as the vent hole of the lodge. Then he let himself fall back with a deep sigh.

"What have you done, Blue Bird?" he demanded. "Running Elk put a great medicine into that bowl of drink. He fasted for three days, and the Underground People told him what to put in it. They told him in a dream."

"I was not told in a dream," said Blue Bird. "Look, Standing Bull. Here is the sign of the god on my head."

She touched the owl feather, and the chief fell silent, staring with wide eyes. The squaw who had not left the teepee, crouching in a corner, held a child gathered close to her inside the grasp of each arm; she seemed to be seeing a terrible ghost instead of the pretty face of Blue Bird.

And here came a small tumult, and then Running Elk strode into the lodge with armed men behind him. He was in a frightful rage. His skinny arm shook as he pointed to the girl.

"Is it true?" he shouted. "Have you spilled out the medicine that I made?"

"Look," whispered the squaw, still crouched in her corner. "The fire is out. She has put out the fire with the evil of the thing she did."

The wood in the fire trench was in fact all black; only a single small head of steam and smoke arose from it.

"The fire is sacred," cried Running Elk, "and you have put it out! The spirits who told me how to make that medicine have stifled the fire with their hands. Those same hands will some night reach for your throat while you sleep and stifle you, also. It will be well for the Cheyennes when that happens."

"Running Elk," said Blue Bird, "you have kept Standing Bull very sick for a very long time. While he lies here, you are the head of the tribe. You don't want him to be well. And that is the word of the god to me."

Running Elk screamed with rage. "You say the thing that is not so!" he cried. "Sweet Medicine would not show his whole face to a woman."

A little murmur of assent came from the braves who had followed the medicine man into the lodge of the chief.

Running Elk went on: "If your act was right and good in the eyes of Sweet Medicine, he would have made the drink you threw away give the fire more brightness. He would have made it a sign. Instead, he caused it to drown out the fire." He turned to the men behind him. "Lay your hands on her and drag her away," he commanded. "We shall have a council to learn how she should be punished. . . . The Underground People are very angry. I can hear their voices inside my ears . . . . They are angry at Blue Bird . . . . They are plucking at my body with their fingernails . . . . Catch hold of her quickly."

Two or three of the warriors stepped forward, but the girl faced them quietly and made no effort to escape.

It was Standing Bull who spoke from his bed in a weary voice: "No matter if she has done wrong. Even if the Underground People put their hands over my mouth and choke me today, she is safe in my lodge."

"Standing Bull is sick. His brain has turned into the brain of a child. Will you take her in your hands?"

One of the braves answered: "She has come from the Sacred Valley. How can we touch her unless she permits us to?"

Blue Bird, looking into the face of the medicine man, shuddered. The constant smile of malice and relaxed old age had turned now into a ghastly rage that worked his features as though with the grasp of a deadly agony.

And then she heard behind her a small cracking or breaking noise. Instantly the squaw of Standing Bull cried out: "A sign! A sign! Look!"

When Blue Bird turned, she saw the thin column of steam and smoke that rose from the embers of the fire had increased to a thickening white arm and from the wood beneath the smoke came the slight noise of the crackling of fire as it grows hotter and eats into the heart of the fuel.

A groan of surprise came from the throats of the warriors.

Standing Bull said: "Now we shall see if my brain is that of a child. Now we shall see if the god uses the hands of Blue Bird to do very wise things . . . . Flame, lift your head if Blue Bird comes from Sweet Medicine. Let us see only one red eye of fire, and it will be enough."

Blue Bird herself, facing the fireplace, dropped on her knees and lifted her hands in prayer, silently.

But Running Elk shouted: "There is nothing of the god in this! Sweet Medicine will not let the fire burn. He speaks in my breast. He commands me to stamp out the heat of the wood . . . ." He strode to the embers, as he spoke, and stamped heavily on them with his moccasined foot.

Two or three of the warriors groaned in fear of this almost sacrilegious act. But the wood, which had been broken down and brought into closer contact by the stamp of the foot, now threw up a much greater cloud of smoke, and in the white mist a golden flickering of fire was seen. It flashed like a signaling hand, far away. It put up an arm of red that was withdrawn again, and now with a cheerful crackling the whole of the embers broke into a strong and steady flame that scattered the smoke above it.

Running Elk drew away with halting, backward dragging steps.

The warriors said in soft voices, one after another: "We have not put out our hands and touched you. We have not harmed you, Blue Bird."

She said nothing. She was continuing her silent prayer.

Chapter Fifteen

Charlie Galway waited three days in the camp. He waited the first day in the hope that he would be able to see something of Blue Bird. But he discovered that the girl had withdrawn from the society of men and women. She went about the lodge of her father in a faintly smiling silence, cooking and cleaning as she always had done. But even Lazy Wolf could not induce her to talk, beyond the speaking of a few words.

It seemed to Galway that either her brain had weakened or she was in the grip of a lasting hysteria. In either case, she was not for him.

Then, on the second and the third day, when he was ready to leave the Cheyenne camp, he was kept there by a continual deluge. The wind shifted into the southwest. All of one night the clouds gathered in increasing piles on the horizon, and the next morning they rolled across the heavens, spilling sheets and torrents of water as they came. There was the smell of the dry earth drinking. The camp turned into a sea of mud. For two whole days and nights, without cessation, the rain fell, and during all that time he had to listen to the chants of the Cheyennes in praise of Sweet Medicine, who first had answered their prayers by filling the ravine with waters from his Sacred Valley, magic water, and now he had swept up the heaped rain clouds and was giving the water of an entire season in a single downpouring.

But on the third morning the sky cleared. The sun shone. The children ran out to play and their feet made sticky, plopping noises in the mud; the squaws began to take out damp garments and string them up where the sun could dry them. The sides of the lodges were furled up; the entrances were opened; the purifying sun was allowed to strike through everywhere.

On that morning, big Charlie Galway saddled his horses and prepared the packs of the robes and other goods he had obtained from the Indians by trade. Lazy Wolf came to smoke a pipe and watch the work progressing.

He said: "This is a good time for you to be stirring, Charlie. The fact is that the Cheyennes are getting a little restless. Sweet Medicine has been doing so much for them that the warriors want to do something in return."

"Such as lifting the hair of some white men?" asked Galway sharply, turning his head over his shoulder.

"Maybe," said Lazy Wolf. "There's a lot of excitement. Running Elk is in a stew because Blue Bird has taken away some of his trade. She won't try to do a miracle every day, like the re-lighting of the fire in the lodge of Standing Bull, but she's performing a pretty thoroughgoing miracle on Standing Bull himself. He's beginning to eat three times a day and the flesh is coming back on his body as fast as the grass comes in the first warm spring days. His squaws go around laughing with joy like drunken women."

"Do you think that Running Elk was poisoning Standing Bull?" demanded Galway.

"I don't think so. I know so. Just enough poison to keep him from getting better. Not enough to kill him. Because, the moment he died, another war chief would be chosen, and Running Elk wouldn't be the single head of the tribe."

"If you knew that, why didn't you tell some of the lesser chiefs?"

"Because there's no use trying to talk down a medicine man. If I accused him, he'd do a devil dance and find out that I was a bad influence in the tribe, and they'd probably skin me alive. But Standing Bull is getting back his strength, and Running Elk is having chills and fevers at the thought of what will happen when the war chief is back on his feet. By this time, Standing Bull knows why he was sick such a long time. And he's saying nothing, but waiting for a chance to get even. That's why we'll all be on the warpath before long."

"I still don't follow it. Civil war, you mean?"

"There's never civil war among the Cheyennes. But Running Elk is sure to try to build up his reputation again, and that means the warpath. He'll get an inspiration, one of these days, and take all the best of the young braves away on a war expedition against the Pawnees, or even against the whites, I suppose. In war days the Indians are a pretty tricky lot. It's better for you to get away and keep away."

"I'm doing that," agreed Galway. "But tell me, man, what makes you stay on here, now that your daughter has gone a little out of her head?"

"She hasn't gone out of her head," said the trader. "She simply feels that she's got something up her sleeve. Like a woman who knows that she's going to have a baby, or something like that. Something that men don't know anything about."

* * * * *

Charlie Galway told himself that he would head straight back for the town of Witherell with the news that the Cheyennes were about to be up and stirring before long. But he could not help changing the course of his journey until he was close to the entrance of the Sacred Valley. And there he halted, to brood over a number of strange events.

There was some means of communication between the Valley of Death and the Sacred Valley, of course. For he had seen Blue Bird led into the first valley, and later on she had walked calmly out of the second. A god, she said, had carried her from one place to the other. Some agency, but not a god.

As for what actually had happened, no court in the land would believe a word of her testimony; it was a very dizzy business about being carried up to heaven, and all that sort of thing. But, in the end, how had she managed to get from one rockbound valley into the next?

Other things had happened. Very strange things. The business of the owl feather, of course, was the purest nonsense. But why had the girl come walking out of the Sacred Valley in that strange trance that still persisted? What had induced her to defy the strength of the great medicine man?

But first, and above all, if Rusty Sabin had mined gold somewhere in this country — if the source of the gold was unknown — if he had been the only man to enter the valley and come out again alive . . .

Charlie Galway turned with his pack horses right into the ravine that entered the Sacred Valley. He rode last, to drive the horses before him. He carried a pair of loaded revolvers in the saddle holsters, had a rifle balanced in his hands, and his nerves were filled by apprehension to an incredible tensity and accuracy.

So he came with his outfit into sight of the Sacred Valley, and his breath stopped. It had been newly washed by the rain. The big trees rolled like bright clouds above the deep pastures. The river ran with a small song down the center of the valley, and now from the farther end of the valley he could see the white face of the waterfall whose mysterious murmurings and chantings, heard at the mouth of the Sacred Valley, were construed into words and answers by the Cheyennes, when they came to consult the oracle.

The eye of the trader grew brighter and brighter. This naturally fenced and reserved valley was the sort of a place in which he could settle for the rest of his days. It was the sort of a place in which he would settle. When he took a wife, he would come here.

As for the Cheyennes — well, the matter would have to be settled with them, but sooner or later, at any rate, a war was sure to come that would sweep the red men farther back on the prairies.

And then he came to a little rabbit run in the grass and in the middle of the small trail was set a trap. Startled, big Charlie Galway jerked up his head and stared around him.

Was there a god in the Sacred Valley? Well, no god had made that trap but a mere man. He got down and examined the thing. It was well enough done, but he himself could have made a better contraption, he felt. A very average sort of a man had made that trap, in fact. And Charlie Galway was not average. He stretched his arms a little to reassure himself with the sense of the muscles that robed his shoulders with power. Here he was, armed to the teeth, to set himself against a man or men who made silly little rabbit traps instead of shooting such game as they required.

A scattering rush of little hoofs — and a herd of antelope broke out of covert and flashed across the meadows of brown, sun-cured grasses. They did not run far. As he lifted his rifle to shoot, he was checked by the multiplicity of the targets. For they stopped only a short distance away and turned toward him, every one of them!

Suddenly Charlie Galway began to laugh. These animals had no fear of man.

Well, he would teach them different ideas. Before long, he would have their hides cured and ready for the market. He would have their meat dried. The simplest thing in the world to build a barrier across the mouth of the valley.

As for the present inhabitant or inhabitants — well, they would have to talk to his rifle. And he knew who would win that argument.

He gave up the thought of shooting game. That could wait until he was ready to eat. No matter where he paused, there would be a full meal of fresh meat waiting, in whatever direction he turned his rifle.

Sacred Valley? It was, in fact, a sort of hunter's paradise.

He came to the lake. It was much smaller, now, than the dimensions to which it had been spread by the dam. Most of the big stones of the dam had been washed and rolled away. There was only a small body of water and on every side of it a muddy stretch streaked and worn by the rush of the water when the dam was broken.

He could understand now, and perfectly, how the thing happened and how the great rush of water had been loosed into the lower ravine of the river. The moving of a few big stones — and then the pouring of the loosened water would complete the rest of the work and let the whole lake rush off down the ravine.

Charlie Galway, sharpening his eyes, scanned the valley on all sides. But still there was no sign of a dweller. He would have to be on the look-out for the twang of a bowstring and an arrow discharged from one of the many coverts.

Then, to the side, in the midst of the muddy margin of the lake, just beginning to crust over with a dry upper layer, he saw a thin streak of something that flashed — something that flashed with a rich yellow color.

Charlie Galway, instantly, was off his horse and floundering out into the mud. He reached that yellow streak — no it was not the one toward which he had started. Instead, it was a smaller color nearer at hand. And there were others — streaks and little patterns of the same rich yellow. He scooped up some of the mud. In a rivulet he washed it clear. In the palm of his hand remained a dozen little specks or tiny pebbles of a heavy yellow metal.

Out of a handful of mud, this much gold, gold, gold!

He wanted to swallow it. The passion of joy made him throw back his head and look toward the sky with an instinctive out-swelling of joy, and of gratitude.

But God had nothing to do with this great discovery. It was the work of his own sharp brain and his brave heart that had enabled him to find the way to the source of Rusty Sabin's wealth.

Here — with his single hand — to wash out a week's wages — why, what could a man do with a proper mining pan?

And it was his — all his — as soon as the setter of traps, the keeper of the valley was out of the way.

Chapter Sixteen

There had to be a death. Charlie Galway waded out of the mud again and got back to his horses, where the pack animals were tearing at the long grass of the pasture land.

There had to be a death, and that must be the man who had made and set the rabbit trap in the grass. Galway herded his horses loosely together and drove them around the edge of the lake until, on the upper margin of the lake, he was able to see, half hidden among the trees, the outlines of a house, thatched at the top, built apparently of some sort of bricks.

He could not have been more amazed if he had seen a Greek temple in the midst of a strange wilderness. A house built of bricks!

He approached it by making, in the first place, a wide circle. Nothing living responded to him. Nothing showed within or outside the place.

At last, he stalked the house and peered in at a door. What he saw inside was a quite empty interior where there had been placed a few chairs made of withes and willows after the Indian style but according to the white man's idea of convenience. This startled the observer almost more than the fact that a house of flat bricks had been found at the end of nowhere.

He turned back to stare about him. Still there was no observer anywhere near him. No matter how he squinted into the brush, he could see no shadowy outlines of a lurking form, no glint of a weapon.

At last he went into the house. The packages of dried rabbit's meat, the harvested bushels of oats were such preparations as any Indian might make against winter. The bed of woven willow rods, more supple than any mattress, was of Indian manufacture, also. But this manufacture was cruder, he thought, than he had ever seen coming from the hands of Indian women.

The chairs were undoubtedly meant for a white man's idea of convenience, and what Indian architect since the beginning of time would have designed and partially constructed the big fireplace and chimney? This was a white man's notion. But, on the other hand, where was there to be found a white man who would attempt such tasks as these without the slightest evidence of steel tools or weapons?

He examined the boards of the floor. They were half logs that had been worked, apparently, by fire and dull edges. Steel could not have been used to batter the wood half smooth, in this fashion. He found in a corner a clumsy fish spear with a bone trident. He found a stone axe, the head lashed onto the wooden haft by the use of tendons, wound and rewound.

This he took across his knees, sitting in one of the homemade chairs, and studied at length. It was made of flint, in the head, and the stone was not properly bound to the haft. He had seen more than one stone tomahawk and other stone implements of the Indians, but none had been fastened so clumsily. It was an improvised tool, he would have said.

And yet what man would have made such things?

No Indian, he could swear, would have had the thought, the patience to build such a house. And yet what white man would even have attempted such a task without the proper materials at hand? The bricks of the walls, for instance, were misshapen — or, rather, they were shaped as though by hand, and not from any mold.

He was still considering when, it seemed to him, the light inside the room darkened a little.

He sat up straight, considering even this slight alteration of his environment. A moment later, the light was again bright. But it seemed to him that a faint, whispering sound came from behind him. At that, he leaped from his chair and tried to whip up the long, heavy rifle to his shoulder.

As he turned, he saw a man with long, flying red hair that streamed across his shoulders, and a face set for stern effort. Vaguely he realized, in the swirl of the attack, that it was Rusty Sabin who leaped in at him.

But that could not be. Rusty Sabin was dead . . . .

He fired, but, as his hand pulled the trigger of the rifle, the reaching hand of Rusty knocked the barrel of the rifle up and to the side.

He had missed. And in return he saw the blade of a knife flash before his eyes.

Yet it was not the point that struck home. At the last instant, he saw the flashing blade turn. It was the heavy butt that struck him between the eyes and felled him to the door.

He was not completely stunned, but his mind was half asleep as he felt the other lean over him and take away the revolver that he had belted on his hip. His hunting knife, similarly, was removed. His rifle, which had crashed to the floor, was lifted.

Then a hand was laid on his neck and remained there for a moment.

At last Rusty's voice said: "You are living, Galway. Stand up, therefore."

Galway rose. He was staggering a little. The room spun before his eyes. He lifted a hand and wiped the blood from his face, for the weight of the blow had split the flesh between his eyes.

Rusty said: "Sit down . . . there."

Galway took a chair and waited.

The whole thing was growing obvious. Only a man who was neither Indian nor white could have done the things that he had witnessed in the valley — and was not Sabin the white Indian?

"You came here to rob the Sacred Valley," said Sabin.

"I didn't come here to rob," said Galway. "I just came to look around."

"I watched you when you ran into the mud of the lake," answered Sabin. "And when I saw you there, I read your mind. I know that the white men love gold, gold. You steal and murder to gain it. Gold. I knew your heart when I saw you in the lake, washing the gold with your hands."

"Aye," answered Galway. "When I saw that, I was sure that I was the first man in the valley. I didn't dream that there was another man here before me."

"No?" asked Rusty.

"It was only after that I saw your house, here."

"I watched you all the time," said Rusty. "You moved like a stalking cat. You had your rifle ready, and you were prepared to kill. Is that true?"

"You take a man in a strange country," said Galway, "and he has to look out. A man that's seen gold is going to be pretty light on his feet and pretty sharp in the eye."

Rusty nodded, watching him. "What am I to do with you?" he asked.

"I'll tell you what I think," said Galway. "We could make a partnership."

"Partnership?"

"What I mean is this. I wouldn't mean to get an equal share. You're here on the ground. You found the gold. You ought to have most of it. But you take and develop a place like this and you need help. You need men and money. You need somebody inside to oversee things. You need an outside agent to keep handling the transportation. There's gotta be somebody to command the trains that haul the loot away. There's gotta be more than one man on the inside of this work. Well, you're the main head of everything. But why shouldn't I be the second one?

"There's a good-size fortune in meat and hides standing on foot in this place, and then we could get in some plows and horses or mules and check the valley off into fields and start putting it to some use."

"Do you think it is not of some use now?" asked Rusty.

"I dunno what use it is. Do you?"

"It is the garden of a god. It cannot be used by men, unless they are his priests," said Rusty calmly. "Because you have entered the house of Sweet Medicine, you must die."

He handled the revolver that he had taken from Galway. The calmness with which he spoke and the peculiar steadiness of his eye shot horror through the blood of Galway.

"But look here, Sabin," he said, "you're not the fellow to murder a man."

"I won't murder you," said Rusty. "I'll give you a gun to use. There's another revolver in the holster on the saddle of your horse. You can have that."

Galway could draw breath again. "I'll fight it out with you, then," he said. "I see you're a right sort of man, Sabin. Everybody always has said that you're a right square sort. Why the people in Witherell didn't treat you better that night, I don't know. You seen me talking for you and Standing Bull."

"Did you talk for us?" asked Rusty.

Galway swallowed. The naïve childishness of this man in some ways, and his insight in other matters, made a combination that he could not understand. He continued his lie quickly: "I did what I could. When they started shooting, I knocked up the muzzles of some of the guns. I don't say that I saved your life for you. But I tried to help."

"Ah? Were you a friend to me?" Rusty sighed. "Tell me with an honest heart. Were you a friend?"

"You can see what I did," said Galway. "I'll tell you what. It sort of made me sick to think of a fine big fellow like Standing Bull being strung up for a thing that likely he didn't do. And when you threw in with the Indian, I wanted to help the pair of you."

"I seem to remember," said Rusty, "that you were not altogether a friend, that night. But I may be wrong. If I kill you, Galway, it's not because I really wish to harm you."

"Then what's all the talk about fighting it out with the guns?"

"You have come into the house of the god, and therefore you must die."

"How do you know," said Galway, "that Sweet Medicine doesn't want me in here? Why was I led inside the Sacred Valley if Sweet Medicine didn't want me here?"

"He will make that clear to us when we shoot at one another," said Rusty. "I have done many bad things. It may be that I shall die and that you will serve the god in my place. Perhaps he has brought you here to be his servant."

"You don't put a whale of a lot of trust in him?" asked Galway.

"I trust him as far as I can know him," said Rusty. "But how can a man know the whole will of a god? If I were a good man, my heart should be filled with happiness to live in the house of Sweet Medicine and to see his face every day. But I find myself in pain many times. I grow hungry for my people. The voice of the waterfall is not enough. It may be that my unhappiness displeases the god. Are you ready to take the other gun?"

Galway stood up. His head was clear. His eye was bright. However excellent a shot Rusty might have been in former days, he hardly could be in practice after all this length of time without guns. But with Galway an hour a day of target practice was religiously observed.

He walked out of the doorway ahead of Rusty and went straight to his saddle horse. He pulled the Colt out of the holster, and he could have laughed as he faced Rusty. The fellow was crazy, with his talk about the Indian god. And in the hands of a crazy man the treasures of the Sacred Valley could not be left. There was a sort of fate in this — a fate that had led him to the valley so that its resources should be properly exploited. History would not forget the name of Charlie Galway. A rough man, but a fellow who did things worthwhile.

When he saw Rusty standing at perfect ease, with the Colt hanging loosely down in his hand, a slight pity touched Galway.

In that man, he felt, there was a purity of mind such as could not be found in others, but there was the simplicity of a savage, also, and the simple creatures must fall before the more complex brains of civilized man.

"When you're ready, tell me," said Rusty carelessly.

"What sort of a signal do you want?" asked Galway.

"I don't know. Whatever you please. When that bull bellows again from the buffalo herd, for instance?"

"Ready, then," said Galway.

He stood tense, his weight a little forward on one foot, and Rusty, at ease, awaited the next booming thunder from the throat of the bull on the farther side of the lake.

It came, a vast, thick, confused note. The two guns leaped in the hands of the fighters. They exploded almost on an instant, or rather the two shots were so close together that they made one detonation.

Something whirred past the ear of Rusty. His own bullet knocked the gun from the hand of Galway and flung the heavy revolver back against his face. Galway, knocked prone on his back, lay senseless.

And Rusty turned straight toward the cave of Sweet Medicine.

"Your hand turned the bullet, oh, Father," he said. "Your hand struck the blow for me. You are not angry with your servant, then?"

He went to the place where big Charlie Galway lay. The man breathed. Rusty lifted his Colt and took aim between the eyes. And at that moment they opened and looked wildly upward. The gun sank in the hand of Rusty. He stretched out an arm toward the cavern in the cliff.

"Give me a sign, Father!" he called.

There was no stir at the mouth of the cave. There was only a vaguely ringing echo flung back from the face of the rock.

Chapter Seventeen

Because only that hollow, booming echo came back from the cliff, Charlie Galway rode in safety out of the Sacred Valley that day. He had one rifle and one revolver with him. The other guns remained with Rusty. He sat on White Horse at the mouth of the ravine and called after Galway: "If you should come again, remember Sweet Medicine! The god will strike you down the moment your foot enters the gate of the ravine. Or he may use my hand to destroy you!"

Charlie Galway made no answer. The pain of his wounded face blurred his thoughts somewhat, but he already had mapped in his mind the plan of his campaign. In the Sacred Valley there was a half-Indian fanatic who worshipped the god of a barbarous tribe, a fanatic now armed to the teeth and on his guard. The next intruder certainly would die the moment Rusty could put a bullet through him.

But Rusty was a very small barrier compared with the treasure to which he blocked the way. If Charlie Galway could not master the valley by himself, he would find a way in which he could raise up a whole army, if necessary. They would break through into the golden land in spite of all the Cheyennes in the world. He knew, in Witherell, a choice selection of hardy fellows to whom the sight of a handful of gold dust would bring visions of a brighter land than paradise.

A hundred of those frontier gallants would cut their way to the Sacred Valley and into it and out again with their treasure in spite of the Cheyennes — if all went well.

The mind of Galway did not dwell on the fact that this would be a shabby return to a very generous enemy. He was capable of gratitude, but it never could be in him a feeling as strong as the pain from his wounded face. When he thought of Rusty Sabin, he thought of a madman. And madmen don't count in this world of Galways.

And yet there remained in the mind of Galway a powerful picture of that moment when he opened his eyes and saw above him the leveled revolver in the hand of Sabin. Why the bullet had not been fired he could not imagine. And yet he guessed, vaguely, that there was something in the nature of Sabin superior to his own world. Because he guessed this, a sullen anger began to rise in his soul.

It was to increase, rapidly, each time he reflected on the adventure of the Sacred Valley until he began to feel, in the end, a sort of righteous indignation when he recalled how frankly, how almost nobly, he had suggested a partnership to Rusty, a partnership in which Rusty could have retained three-quarters of the spoils.

And, again, it began to seem to Galway that he was performing an act on behalf of all mankind if he scared the dog out of the manger. He was only concerned in securing himself ten shares of the spoils, as captain of the invading army. But, oh, if he could have had the looting of the Sacred Valley all to himself. That vision of splendid hope, lost forever, would haunt him to the end of his life.

* * * * *

In the Sacred Valley, from day to day, Rusty Sabin went on with the building of his house, working constantly at the erection of the massive fireplace that was to crown his labor. He had better tools, now. Before the departure of Galway, he had helped himself to some of the trader's possessions, particularly to a heavy axe, the back of whose head made an excellent hammer; he had also some rope, ammunition, a rifle, a revolver, a saddle. He had an adze for the shaping of planks, and, above all, he had a saw. The saw was the treasure beyond price.

But although he busied himself constantly, his days were not happy. It was in vain that the valley turned from brown to green. It was in vain that the great night owl, every evening or every morning, stooped from the lip of the cave and swept down to take from his hand the sacrifice of the rabbit. Even when he worked himself to a state of exhaustion, he could not sleep well at night.

There remained in his heart a sort of weary sorrow, an emptiness that he could not understand. He told himself that it was an uneasiness based on the manner in which he had allowed Galway to escape from the valley.

It was true that Galway had sworn never to return, but the oaths of the white men never weighed half so heavily in their minds as a single ounce of yellow gold. And Galway knew that the Sacred Valley possessed a soil rich with the metal. Could it be that he would stay away, or would he return with companions?

Sweet Medicine, of course, could protect his own. And yet when Sabin thought of the force of disciplined white fighting men, well armed, trained, obedient to command, ready to fight to the death, he felt, with a shudder, that even the strength of a god would hardly be enough to defeat them. His own adopted people, the Cheyennes, were brave as brave. A single warrior chosen at random from among the red men would be almost certain to dispose with ease of a single white man. But with numbers came a mysterious change.

A score of Indians might be baffled by three resolute whites each guarding the back of the other, all patiently determined, fighting on calmly and intelligently even when no hope appeared.

The splendid rush and sweep of the Indian charge was turned back by the rock-like stubbornness of the whites; the keen edge was turned by the hard face of the stone. Ten white men, well in order, even nine novices with one experienced leader, might move guardedly across the plains and beat off a hundred selected braves. And therefore if Galway loosed against the Sacred Valley a wave of armed white men, it would need the strength of the god at its full to turn them back. He trusted the god, but feared the future.

In this odd unhappiness of Rusty, in this emptiness of spirit, there was another cause for grief. The memory of Blue Bird kept walking up and down the valley at his side. And most of all he remembered her as she had sat on the back of White Horse on that last morning, between smiling and sorrow.

Maisry Lester occupied his mind every day, also. But the recollection of her was a different matter. It was something more important, more beautiful, but almost as removed from actuality as are the ghosts of the dead.

His people had cast him out and he never could see her again. But with the Cheyennes it was different, and many a day, when he rode White Horse down the valley at high noon, he would hear the chant of a prayer come echoing up the hollows of the ravine.

They were not answered by the waterfall's echoes alone, now. Sometimes he put his face close to the hollows of the rocky face of the cliff and called out words in a melancholy, straining voice, words that could be put together to make one of several meanings. It was not that he wanted to be mysterious, but, when he listened to the prayers, he usually felt some immediate emotion that, he felt, was communicated directly to him from the god.

So, when he heard a young lad crying out at the mouth of the ravine, he listened and made out, clearly, the words of the appeal.

"Sweet Medicine, shall I be strong for the torment of the initiation? Shall I be able to drag the big buffalo head tied to the flesh of my raw shoulders with the thongs? Shall I scream out like a woman or shall I be strong and silent like a man? Sweet Medicine, tell me if I shall be ashamed. Be merciful!"

And Red Hawk, remembering the shame of that initiation that he had not been able to face, answered: "The known face is not terrible. The day is a friend . . . the night is the terror. To the boy, manhood is a mystery. To the man, boyhood is sleep and happy dreams remembered. But to Sweet Medicine the young and the old are of one age. If you take the step into manhood, you take the step with pain. All the pain you have known will help you."

And again on a day he heard a chanting of many men and then the hoarse, familiar voice of Running Elk, saying: "Sweet Medicine, you have sent water to us out of your own hand. You have given rain to make the world green once more. Now we are going to show that we are your children and love you. We are going to get scalps and sacrifice them to you. Not the scalps of the Sioux or the Pawnees. We are going to bring you better scalps. We are going to bring you the scalps of white men and long-haired scalps of white women and the soft hair of children. Give us a token."

Then he answered: "The horses are weary. The warriors search the edge of the sky with searching eyes. The smoke of the white man rises. Happy is the brave who returns to the town of the Cheyennes. Happy is the warrior whose skin is not beaten by the rain until it rots like old grass."

He was very troubled. It had seemed to him, as he spoke, that perhaps on this occasion he was speaking a little more for himself, a little less for Sweet Medicine, in trying to avoid the war between white men and Indians.

He remained in the Sacred Valley until sunset, every moment more and more disturbed. And at last he saddled White Horse and took rifle and revolver with him. He felt that he was being drawn forward by a force like that of a great wind, an irresistible impulse. And so he rode straight out of the valley, past the towering rock pillars of the gate.

Chapter Eighteen

In the camp of the Cheyennes, there remained a reaction after the departure of the war party like the bubbling, swirling wake that passed over water behind a speeding boat. So in the village of the Cheyennes the enthusiasm of the people did not subside at once but, instead, expended itself in various small ways.

At night, the young men with musical instruments that made howling noises went to serenade their ladies. The dogs poured back and forth through the camp chasing imaginary wolves with a terrible clamor from dark to dawn. The old men sat down cross-legged to tell stories of the prowess of their youth, and the young men were overcome by the war spirit and yearning because they had been left behind so that at any moment of the day or the night they were impelled to leap up with a war cry and do a war dance in which with a war club or an axe they brained airy enemies by the score and took hundreds of invisible scalps.

That evening, half a dozen of the braves were seized by enthusiasm at the same moment and began to yelp and whoop with such energy that the dogs of the Cheyennes caught the enthusiasm of the idea and started to chase the imaginary wolves and fight over the imaginary bones again.

Standing Bull heaved himself up on his elbows and remained in this posture, half risen from his willow bed. Now that he made the effort it was possible to see how nearly he had recovered from his illness. The big shoulder muscles were filling out. Across his breast the traces of strength were reappearing. His skinny shanks were swelling day by day with the commencement of the huge power of his ordinary health.

Blue Bird said: "He is only halfway back to earth from the Happy Hunting Ground, but already he wants to be taking scalps and counting the coup."

The two squaws of the brave smiled and nodded. They would not have dared to make such a remark about their famous husband, but they were brave enough to agree with that newly privileged person in the camp, one who herself had passed through an unearthly adventure.

Standing Bull looked up to the girl with a smile and watched the owl feather that trembled continually in her hair.

"What is happening now, Blue Bird?" he asked. "Have they sighted an enemy? Are they surrounding him?"

"They have come to the end of the day," said the girl, still smiling. "They are tired. Their horses are white with dried sweat. Their stomachs are empty. There is only a little stale water left in the water bags. They sit about and chew some parched corn. They look about them toward the ends of the earth. The world is a big place and honor is hard to find in it. Clouds are in the sky. It will rain on them before the morning."

"No," said Standing Bull. "They are pressing on through the hills. They see before them the town of the white men. They creep forward. As the night begins, they rush suddenly forward. The white men sit inside their wooden lodges and eat, and blind themselves with the light of their lamps. The Indians rush like a storm on them. The white men run out with guns. They are shot down, the tomahawk is in their brains, their red scalps are torn from their heads!

"Ah, my people! You forget what Red Hawk so often told you . . . that Witherell is not the chief city of the whites, that they are more numberless than the buffalo in the prairies. For this first blow you strike, you will be smitten a hundred times. All the

Cheyennes will feel the strength of the white warriors. They will come by thousands, and every man will carry a rifle that shoots straight. My tribe will be lost."

"Will they go so far?" asked the girl, staring. "Will they go even to the town of Witherell, Standing Bull?"

"They will go wherever the evil brain of Running Elk can lead them," said the war chief. "He knows that before long I shall be able to ride a horse, and, when that happens, he will be no longer the head chief of the Cheyennes unless he does some great thing. That is the reason he takes three hundred warriors, well-armed, and rides away. He dreams of a great battle. The heart of the bad man never is small."

"The wooden lodges of the white men are very strong," said the girl. "Sometimes they are made of heavy walls, and there are loopholes through which the guns can be fired. Every house is like a fort."

"Suppose that the grass is lighted, and the flames sweep down over the town? The white men run out like frightened rabbits. The Cheyennes are before them in the streets, killing them by scores. But for every white man who dies, ten Indians shall be shot down later on. That is the word of Red Hawk. *Ah hai*, Blue Bird. If he were alive . . . as he is dead . . . he would be able to stop the madness of my people. No other man could do it."

An immensity of sorrow, a sense of doom covered the mind of the girl. All that she had seen inside the Sacred Valley must remain nameless. She could not even say to Standing Bull that his friend was not dead, but living. Or was it life indeed that Red Hawk had inside the Sacred Valley? If he were brought into the light and the air of common places, might he not be utterly dead and a ghost?

She began to tremble. She began to taste again the life in the Sacred Valley.

Afterward, she made medicine.

She did it very simply, as one who could be sure that the Sky People would hear her voice and give her wisdom. In her father's lodge, she picked up a handful of dust and blew on it.

He sneezed and looked up from the book that he was reading by the light of a lantern with glass sides — a miracle to the Cheyennes.

"What's the matter, Blue Bird?" he asked her.

She raised her free hand to let him see that she was conversing with the gods. Then, with lowered eyes, she counted the small pebbles that remained in her palm, some of them almost too small to glisten.

The number was odd. It meant that the gods wanted her to complete a task. What could the task be? Why, the very one that Standing Bull had named to her.

Her father was saying: "You and I are going on a journey, Blue Bird. You're getting a little out of hand, what with all this medicine making, and dust blowing, and stewing of herbs. There's always a bad smell in the lodge, and, besides, I'm disturbed by all the women who come with their sick children to you and ask you for cures. Do you think that the Sky People really are telling you how to help the sick?"

She looked down again at the pebbles in her hand, and then closed the fingers over the little stones.

She knew, now, what course she would have to take.

She got up suddenly, and left the lodge with bowed head. As she stood under the stars again, it was revealed to her what she must do.

From among the horses tethered near the teepee, she took the big colt with one blue and one black eye, the fiercest, the strongest, the wildest of the horses belonging to rich Lazy Wolf. When she returned inside the lodge, she took her saddle from the post from which it hung.

"Where are you away now, Blue Bird?" asked Lazy Wolf.

Instead of answering, she picked up a small leather bag filled with parched corn, and a light rifle that her father had bought especially for her. When she reached the entrance to the teepee, Lazy Wolf called after her: "Confound it, Blue Bird, tell me what's up now! I'm getting a little tired of all this conversation with Sky People. Try talking for a while with your father and you may find one or two good ideas tucked away inside his old brain."

Her heart was pinched. She wanted to answer. It was her sacred duty as a daughter to answer the questions of her father, but a vow that held her was more binding still — she must not utter a syllable until she stood again at the awful entrance to the Sacred Valley.

She heard him muttering as she saddled the young stallion.

Her heart went out to him, but the vow laid a cold finger on her lips and kept her silent.

Now the horse was equipped. She mounted and rode slowly through the village. As she came out from among the teepees, from all the night noises of the town, she saw hanging in the east the thin, curved knife of the new moon.

She went on. The glimmering lights of the village grew pale behind her. And then a sudden rush of hoof beats came roaring toward her and the shouting voices of young men of the night guard who rode around and around the town. Not another woman among the Cheyennes would have abided that charge.

Only Blue Bird rode straight on at the usual dog-trot of an Indian pony.

They swept away. The dust from the hoofs of their horses stung her nostrils. Then she was alone in the night.

Chapter Nineteen

At the gates of the Sacred Valley, for a long hour Blue Bird cried to the god, and the only answer she heard was the whisper of the water running down the bed of the ravine, and the far-off chanting of the waterfall at the other end of the valley.

Wiser people than she, perhaps, could have construed that echo into words with a meaning, but Blue Bird merely withdrew to one side and lay face down on the ground, pressing the palms of her hands against it, praying to the Underground People. And as she lay there, the dawn began, slowly, a light streaming gradually up around the edges of the great bowl of the sky.

She heard, at last, a light footfall on the rocks and, turning her head, was aware of a great elk, a king of his kind, standing at the entrance of the Sacred Valley. His head was lifted so that the great tree of horns sloped well back over his body. In spite of size and sleek weight, he had the look of a creature with winged heels.

The girl sat up, trembling with awe. This was the manner in which the souls of the dead heroes approached the Sacred Valley. Here was some famous warrior, clad in a new form, standing on the verge of paradise. The elk turned his head, saw her, and bounded straightforward through the gates of the valley.

Blue Bird arose, her eyes shining.

In some far place on the prairies a whole tribe, perhaps, was lamenting for the death of a war chief; the voices of the women were screeching to the sky, their faces were marred by their own nails, their hair was cut short and clotted with dust as they howled. How could they know that in a form so new and splendid the brave man's soul was entering the earthly heaven of the Sacred Valley?

She went again to the mouth of the valley and called out her prayer, and again there was no answer.

Always her prayer was the same: to send Red Hawk out from the Sacred Valley so that the war between the whites and the Cheyennes might be averted. The empty silence of the ravine at last weighed down her mind. She turned away full of uncertainty.

Red Hawk seemed to her half man and half god, who had passed through death into a higher life though he still moved and breathed upon the earth. He it was who should, as Standing Bull declared, hold back the Indians and perhaps check the white men.

How could he be drawn forth from the Sacred Valley on that errand of peace?

Then, suddenly, bitterly, she remembered the white girl, the blue eyes, the beauty, the smiling. Even the very presence of the god hardly could withhold Red Hawk, if he heard the voice of Maisry Lester calling.

Well, she was no longer Blue Bird, a mere name, a girl of no importance whatever; she was now a famous medicine woman, and for the welfare of her people she must give up her last hope of gaining that happiness of which most women can be sure. She felt such pain that she put both hands over her heart for a moment and closed her eyes. Then she laid her course straight across the plains toward the distant town of Witherell.

It was the twilight of a day when she came to the edge of the hills and looked down into the shallow, dimly lighted bowl of the town. The English that her father had taught her was not very good, not very extensive, but it was enough to enable her to ask her way to the house of Maisry Lester. She remembered that other time and that other town that she had visited in order to see the white girl. She remembered sadly, and shook her head. Then she rode her tired horse down the slope.

She had been remembering all through her journey the details of wisdom that the Cheyennes had taught her about the whites. These were some of the items.

First, the God of the white man lives too high in the sky to be of any use. He is worshipped by clasping the hands together and rolling up the eyes. He never receives sacrifices that are worth anything, but he is pleased by the moan and howl of a pumping organ. Big wooden teepees are built in his honor, each teepee crowned with a long wooden finger that points toward the sky,

Second, white men are half warriors and half squaws, therefore they are contemptible. They have dim eyes, ears that cannot hear, and no sense of smell. They fight to kill, not to be glorious. They are afraid of the beautiful prairies and lose their way more than children. The sun is not their father and the moon is not their sister. They deform their feet with hard leather, and therefore they neither can run nor walk. Because they are afraid of the sun, they wear heavy things on their heads. They work all day long like squaws, because they are shameless. A white man loves to lie. Wonderful to state, they even lie to one another.

Third, white women keep off their feet as much as possible. They sit a great deal. All the rest of the time they lie down. They keep something in their hands, sewing with a good deal of skill but making silly things of no importance. They are foolish; they love to gather together and giggle. They are cowards; they scream when they see even a mouse. They are cruel; they have been seen to strike little children many blows only because the children make a noise. They are selfish and will not let their men have two women.

Under such main headings, Blue Bird gathered her knowledge of the whites. Among all these people there were two exceptions: Red Hawk and the woman he loved.

Fear began to grow up in the breast of the Indian girl as she entered the first street of the little town. Far away, a whistle blew, with a terrible power, ripping the sky apart, cutting into her brain. She heard men laughing inside a house — bawling, horrible, meaningless laughter. She heard a baby crying, not the sweet, sad sound of a Cheyenne baby that makes the noise "*Ai! Ai! Ai!*" but a disgusting, booing complaint.

Into the sobbing of the baby rattled the harsh voice of a white woman. Blue Bird heard a sound of blows. The baby began to scream. The Indian girl gasped and put her hands over her ears.

She hurried her horse on. Out of the wooden lodges streamed brilliant lights. Unpleasant smells of strange cookery reached her nostrils; she heard metal clatterings. The memory of the Cheyenne village rolled back upon her mind and made her heart ache.

How could Red Hawk have chosen one of these people to be his squaw?

A group of small boys came swirling out into the street, knocking up a cloud of dust, yelling at one another. Blue Bird sighed with relief,

She called out to them: "Will you tell me the place where Maisry Lester lives?"

"Hey! Look-it! It's an Indian gal!" they cried at her.

A shaft of dim lamplight swept over her. She smiled and made a friendly gesture as she asked the question again.

"That way," said one of the lads. "Down there . . . the house with the two trees in front. Hey, who are you? Where did you come from? Are you a Pawnee? Who brought you here?"

Questions are dangerous. She fled from them, galloping her horse, and they pursued her only a little distance before they fell into another dusty swirl of wild play.

So she reached the house and tethered the Indian pony to one of the trees in the front yard. A single light burned at the rear of the place. She looked through the window, touching with her hand curiously the dry ice through which the light shone.

Inside, she saw Maisry Lester, alone, sitting at a kitchen table with her face in her hands. The jealous heart of the Cheyenne was touched.

The brightness of the hair, the slenderness of the hands held her eyes. She wore a dress that seemed to Blue Bird of great worth, for it was a printed calico. The design, the pattern, the color amazed Blue Bird.

She went with soft steps up the back porch and tapped at the door.

"Who is there?" asked a small, weary voice.

Critically Blue Bird examined that voice. She had remembered it too dimly. It was not like the voice of any other white, for it contained a real music.

"It is I!" she called in answer. "It is Blue Bird."

A footfall came suddenly. The door was snatched open. She saw Maisry Lester's face full of startled joy, and then the white girl caught her in her arms. She used that strange white custom of kissing. But it was not very offensive. There was a clean, sweet smell about Maisry that was not unpleasant. It was not as good as the real smoky Indian smell, but it was not horrible, like the odor of most whites.

"Blue Bird, what have you come to tell me?" cried Maisry Lester. "What has brought you so far?"

Now that she had the full picture before her, the Indian girl stared, fascinated, into the blue eyes of Maisry. Blue eyes, she felt, were not as beautiful by half as black or dark brown, and yet there was a sort of shining color in them. The color of the eyes went with the color of the hair, like something painted very skillfully. Her skin was very pale, very pale. She was paler than Red Hawk ever became, even when he had been ill and remained out of the sun for a long time.

"Tell me . . . are you the squaw of some warrior now?" asked the Cheyenne.

"No," said Maisry.

"Do you wait for Red Hawk?" asked Blue Bird.

She saw the white girl blanch and the sight wrung her heart, but also gave her a cruel pleasure.

"Yes," said Maisry.

"Would you wait all your life for a dead man?" asked Blue Bird, more cruelly than ever.

"Yes," said Maisry.

Blue Bird sighed. There was a greatness of spirit in this pale-faced girl. There was something shining about her. She was not tall — she was not strong — but her heart was great.

If ever her voice sounded within the hearing of Red Hawk — no, not even the god could restrain him.

There was a vast urge in Blue Bird to flee away from the house, and never to set eyes on Maisry again. And yet an iron sense of duty held her.

She looked up, and it seemed to her that the beauty of the Sacred Valley unrolled again before her eyes. The god had sent her out from the place. His purpose, perhaps, was to drive her on to the whites, on to Maisry Lester, so that through Maisry the threatened war could be halted. Now the words poured suddenly from her throat: "I can take you to him. He is not dead. He is living, Maisry!"

Chapter Twenty

The trail lay wide and clearly beaten before the eyes of Rusty Sabin. So many scores of warriors with their war ponies and the herd of extra horses driven on by a select number of youth, who for the first time were on the warpath, could not pass over the green of the prairies without leaving unmistakable signs of their passing.

Now and then parties diverged from the main road, the whole body splitting up into small sections that traveled toward varying points of the compass. Then the trailing task became difficult, for each of the smaller bodies attempted to lay a good trail puzzle behind them as soon as they reached a dry ravine or a stream that enabled them to make a problem for a pursuer.

If Rusty lost the trail of the group that he had selected, he would lose the trend of the whole march. Three times he was stopped for a considerable interval by these cunningly constructed puzzles, but on each occasion he was able to work out the solution and ride on.

He was strangely happy. The Sacred Valley, in all its beauty, remained somewhere in his mind as a lonely duty, not as a joyful place. He was away from the god's place, and yet the god had not deserted him. As the dawn was born out of the pale moonlight of that first night, he shot a scurrying rabbit, and, as he dismounted to pick up the body, he felt before he saw the sweep of the broad, familiar wings above him. Looking up, he recognized the huge night owl of the Sacred Valley.

Had he come to accept the sacrifice, even if it were not actually living game? Holding up the limp body, he whistled, and instantly the owl swooped. The talons, like a powerful skeleton hand, grasped the rabbit; the softly rushing wings bore the owl away on high.

Rusty Sabin, looking after the soaring bird, saw it outlined jet black against the moon and the dawn for a moment, then it slid down into the darkness of the prairie. And Sabin laughed happily. This, certainly, was a veritable sign from heaven.

Late that evening he saw the war party of the Cheyennes. They were making a forced march by moonlight, and the long column went over a slight rise of ground, printing themselves as a small black picture against the sky.

Sabin took White Horse at a brisk gallop through an arc that cut across the course of the column. He waited in a hollow until he heard the tramping of the hoofs. He waited with the stallion flat on the ground, almost covered by the tall grass. And at his word, White Horse rose into view with Sabin in the saddle.

The half dozen scouts who preceded the rest were not a hundred steps away when they saw that vision appear from nothingness. Red Hawk's ghost on White Horse — a vision from another world. Their sudden yell of dismay was music to the ears of Sabin.

They had halted. Two of them suddenly turned their ponies about and fled. The rest flung themselves on the ground and began to shout out prayers to the Sky People, prayers to Sweet Medicine.

Sabin rode straight on, at a walk, without turning his head toward the voices of his red people. But his heart was stirred.

Would the war party dare to continue after such a vision had crossed its way? In the distance he made the stallion sink into the depth of the grass. There he left White Horse and returned stealthily until he was close to the camp. The grass was a sufficient shelter.

Peering through the high heads of the grass, he could see the rising of a column of smoke. Out of the distance he could hear the thrumming of a drum. And he understood.

The Cheyennes had halted to make enough of a fire to raise a smoke of sweet grass in which they could purify themselves after the terrible vision of White Horse and the ghost of Red Hawk. After that, perhaps they would attempt to continue the war trail. If so, he would cross their way again.

There was a small wind stirring the grass, and it kept a whispering sound about the ears of Sabin. He never would have heard the other noise that flowed through the sound of the wind; it was the sudden shudder that passed through the body of the stallion that warned him, and the lift and sudden sidewise twist of the head of White Horse.

A snake, perhaps, slipping through the grass?

Well, a snake would turn away from creatures so great. Still, the head of Sabin was turned and his nerves were strung to alertness when he saw, over his shoulder, a shadowy form rising, and the gleam of steel by the pale moonlight. The blow was not a downward cleaving stroke, but a sidelong sweep that was surer to bite home in some part of the body of the enemy. Rusty dropped loosely and lay prone on the ground. The long-bladed knife came into his hand as he heard the tomahawk *whish* over his head. The body of the other lurched toward him, following the stroke, and Rusty turned as a cat turns when it offers its claws to a foe. He stabbed upward and felt the knife blade glide through flesh and grit on bone, and drive deeper.

A great hand gripped Rusty by the hair of the head. He stabbed upward again. The hand lost its power. The tomahawk fell idly in the grass. A loose weight dropped upon Sabin and rolled away from him.

He got to his knees. White Horse was drawing great breaths of horror as it smelled the blood. And stretched before Sabin, vainly struggling to rise again, was a crop-headed Pawnee wolf.

The moonlight slipped like water over the huge flow of muscles that covered his body. Among a nation of big men, he was a giant. He could not handle his own weight, but he intended to strike a last blow. The steel of his knife glistened as he dragged it out of the sheath of fringed leather.

Rusty caught the mighty arm at the wrist. There was no more resistance in that arm than in the muscles of a child.

"Die in peace," said Rusty, "because I take no scalps. I count the coup on you, Pawnee . . . and that is all."

"Ah," muttered the brave, "what bad fortune brought me to you? You are the friend of Sweet Medicine. You are Red Hawk, the great medicine man."

He sat up, clasping his body with one hand. The blood still poured from the terrible wounds he had received. He began to sing the death song, the words coming hoarsely from his throat and with a horrible bubbling in them.

"Sky People, look down carefully. There is not much light . . . I cannot call loudly, but I am Long Arrow the Pawnee. I am the man who killed the white buffalo and sacrificed the skin to you. In the battle, I rode through the line of the Blackfeet and counted coup on a living warrior with a short stick. I stole the thirty horses from the Sioux. And I am the man who stole up in the night on the camp of the Cheyennes and killed the two braves with one knife.

"And I took their scalps and hung them over my fire. Cheyenne hair hangs from the reins of my bridle. The hair of Blackfeet fringes my leggings. You see that I have lived a good life and that I have hope of the Happy Hunting Grounds. And then you led me against Red Hawk.

"I struck with the hatchet and the hand of the god was put in front of it. I struck, and the body of a man turned into air and the stroke was lost. Sweet Medicine turned the tomahawk aside. He guided the knife into my body. The life runs out of me like water downhill. The pool is emptying. Receive me, my fathers."

The big body pitched to the side. Sabin, steadying it with a strong hand, laid back the limp weight of Long Arrow in the grass.

It was a huge-featured face into which he looked, the nose high-arched and the mouth vast and thin-lipped. He never had seen a face more cruel, he thought. But any man who had killed a white buffalo and sacrificed it to the Sky People was, of course, a very good Indian.

It seemed to Sabin that there had been some truth in the death chant of the dying man. Perhaps the invisible hand of Sweet Medicine, so swift that it can reach between a man and his thoughts, had intervened between the tomahawk and its target. Perhaps it was Sweet Medicine who had driven the knife home to the life.

In that case, the body belonged to the god and not to the Cheyennes. For that purpose, and lest any man should claim that warrior or despoil him of his scalp, Rusty took from a little pouch at his belt a single soft owl feather, such as he found in the cave of Sweet Medicine, and tied it with a wisp of Long Arrow's own hair.

The drumbeat in the distance had ended. He heard a rhythmic beating of hoofs and then a confusion of impacts such as are made by the feet of many walking horses. And he saw that the Cheyennes were streaming forward. They had not turned back. They were coming straight along their original course.

The teeth of Sabin gritted together. This was the work of Running Elk, of course. The old medicine man with mischief in his heart had persuaded the braves that the appearance of the ghost was perhaps a good sign, instead of a bad omen. And as the whole procession dipped out of sight in a slight hollow, Rusty again rose from the grass on the back of White Horse.

The train was proceeding straight toward the place where the dead Pawnee scout was lying, and, as it pushed forward over the rise of ground, clear in the moonlight the braves could see White Horse stepping, and a shout of horror arose from many throats.

The forward movement ended. Half of the braves scattered toward the rear, and, as before, a number flung themselves from the saddles to the ground. But Running Elk alone remained steadfast. He kicked his pony forward a short distance, and then reached up both skinny arms as he shouted: "Red Hawk, if you come back from the dead to the living, tell us what the Sky People wish to say to us!"

Sabin, for an answer, lifted his right hand and waved it in the signal that warns a man to go back. Then he turned his head and rode on at a walk, for he felt that the walking horse would be a more apt picture to present the idea of a return from the dead, a mounted ghost.

Behind him, he heard a sudden clamor. When he looked back, he saw that the shouting of Running Elk had put heart in some of the warriors so that they had remounted and pushed forward a little distance to stare along the trail of the ghost.

So they had come on the spot where the dead Pawnee lay. And their yell of triumph turned suddenly into a familiar old chant in praise of Sweet Medicine.

The war party began to pull saddles from their horses. Whatever happened, they would go no farther forward on this night.

Chapter Twenty-One

Blue Bird sat cross-legged and looked for a long time at Maisry. Maisry had started to sit in a chair, but she changed her mind and sat down on the floor, also, not cross-legged, but with her feet on one side and with her right arm supporting her weight.

"You stay in the chair," said Blue Bird.

"No," answered Maisry. "I'll sit the way you do. I'm not above you, Blue Bird."

The Indian smiled. "It is so hard to hate you," she said, "when I want to love you."

"Do you hate me?" asked the white girl.

"There is Red Hawk," said the Cheyenne.

"Yes. There is he," said Maisry.

"You are very calm," said Blue Bird. "You should not be so quiet. Look at me."

"I am looking," said Maisry.

"I am not ugly," said Blue Bird. "Look at me again. Do you see how I am not ugly?"

"I see very well."

"You must remember that, after all, Red Hawk is like a white man more than an Indian. A good Cheyenne brave, when he takes a wife, thinks how many horses she will cost, how many guns and buffalo robes. But a white man never thinks of how much work his wife will be able to do for him. He thinks more about how lovely she is. Do you understand me when I talk Cheyenne like this?"

"Yes, I understand you very well."

"*Ah hai*, Maisry, if your skin had been as dark as mine, we could have loved each other, unless we fell in love with the same man. But you never could be one who might be bought for a price in horses and other things."

"I don't know. I think I could have been bought," said Maisry.

"Maisry, when you say that, you are beautiful."

"When I say it, I feel very sad."

"Perhaps all women must be a little sad if they are to be beautiful."

"Do you think so?"

"Maisry . . . you see that my Cheyenne tongue can say white words?"

"You are half white, you know."

"My blood is all red."

"I know that."

"Do you hear that bird singing?"

"I hear the black bird."

"He is free," said Blue Bird.

"Yes, perfectly free."

"You are not free," said the Cheyenne.

"No?"

"You are not free as Red Hawk is. He is strong and brave and he is as free as the black bird . . . if you would let him be."

"You think that I tie him?" asked Maisry.

"Ah, my sister," said the Indian, "don't you see that you do? Your god is not his god. Your skin is his color, but your heart is not his color. You put birds in cages, but the meadowlark is not in a cage. He is unhappy . . . lines come between his eyes when he is with you. But with me there are no lines between his eyes when he is with me."

"Is he very happy with you?"

"For me he went into the Valley of Death."

"What is that?"

"The Valley of Death. He went into it. The god led him. He carried me from the Valley of Death."

"He carried you in his arms?"

"Yes. In his arms. And through the cave, through the house of the god. I was dead."

"What are you saying, Blue Bird?"

"Through the house of the god."

Her face flamed suddenly. Through the golden obscurity of her skin the color rushed. And Maisry watched carefully.

The Indian girl went on: "Into my dead body he called back the life. The first that I knew was his voice above me. I was in the blue of the Happy Hunting Grounds and he called me back to the earth. His voice called me, praying to Sweet Medicine. Do you know who Sweet Medicine is?"

"Yes. Did Rusty pray for you?"

"That hurts you, doesn't it?"

Maisry drew a quick, deep breath. "You see, Blue Bird, we both love him. We should be honest and tell one another what we think."

"Well," said Blue Bird, "does it hurt you . . . the thing I have just said?"

"Yes," said Maisry, and flushed.

They both were warm of face, staring at each other.

"Do you hate me?" asked Blue Bird.

"Yes," said Maisry. "No," she added.

"*Ai, ai*," said Blue Bird. "Why should we both like him so much? There are many men in the world. There are more men than there are buffalo, Red Hawk says, and yet we find only one."

"Yes," said Maisry, "that is true."

They stared at one another again.

Blue Bird said: "I am going to cry. Cheyennes should not cry. But I cannot help it."

Maisry watched her with a cold face. Blue Bird folded her arms across her face. She made no sound. Her body gently rocked to and fro, and the agony was a silent thing.

Maisry got up and went to her. She sat beside the Indian and put on arm around her. Suddenly the weight of Blue Bird slumped against her.

Blue Bird sobbed openly: "I have seen a great many taller and stronger warriors."

"Yes," said Maisry.

"I have seen great chiefs with many scalps."

"Yes," said Maisry.

"I have seen warriors with the riches of a thousand horses," said Blue Bird.

"Of course you have," answered Maisry. "And men like that have wanted to marry you."

"Yes, they have," said Blue Bird.

"And still you think of him?"

"Yes, I think of him. The god compels me."

They were silent for a moment.

Maisry said: "Are you happier now?"

Blue Bird was drying her eyes. "I have been very weak," she answered. "Now I am better."

"Tell me, Blue Bird, about that Valley of Death . . . do you mean that you were very ill . . . or was it actually the valley where the Cheyennes make their sacrifices?"

"It was that valley," said the Indian.

Maisry reached out a hand toward her and left the gesture suspended in air for a moment.

"He carried you out of that? But how could he?" she asked.

"The god is his companion. He can do everything that the god wishes him to do. I can't talk any more about it or Sweet Medicine will freeze up my blood and turn me to dead stone.

Maisry, there is another valley near the Valley of Death. It is the Sacred Valley where Sweet Medicine lives.

"I went to the entrance to that valley, just a little while ago, and called to the god and called to Red Hawk and begged them to stop the Cheyennes on the warpath and keep them from fighting with the white people. The god would not hear me . . . Red Hawk would not hear me. . . ."

"Is that where he lives?"

"I can't tell you that," said the Indian. "I can't tell you anything I know about that. I can only say that if you went to the Sacred Valley and called, surely Red Hawk would come out in answer to your voice. I am only a dark-faced Indian. It is you that he loves. He would come and he could turn back the Cheyennes from the warpath. Will you go with me?"

Maisry, listening with eyes of desperate interest, exclaimed: "But the two of us . . . to ride alone through an Indian country . . . !"

"There are not many Pawnees. Most of them are Cheyennes, and I could make you safe from all the Cheyenne warriors. Look . . . you have a very good horse."

She pointed out the window toward the pasture in which stood a blood-red mare, one of those rare bays whose skin seems actually to be dyed by the life stream.

"I have a good pony, also," said Blue Bird. "Who could catch us, if we traveled mostly at night? Will you come, Maisry?"

The thought of the prairie seemed to Maisry like the thought of a wild sea, filled with danger. But every day of her life in Witherell had been a barren wilderness since the death of her father. And suddenly lifting her head she said: "Yes, I'll go."

"Good!" cried Blue Bird. "Now? Will you come now?"

"Now . . . this moment," said Maisry.

Chapter Twenty-Two

An ounce of gold could buy a great many things in the town of Witherell, but on the equipment of his expedition Charlie Galway expended the last speck of gold dust he had gotten in the Sacred Valley and from the robes he had traded with the Cheyennes. He spent so much organizing the outfit that people no longer referred to him as Charlie. He now was "Captain" Galway, a title that he could keep the rest of his life if he used a little discretion.

He spent his money freely, not that he was the sort of a man who used possessions with a free hand, but because he was sure that for every cent he spent now, he would have a hundredweight of gold in the future. He had drawn together exactly twenty-five men for the expedition. His advertising had been unlike that which ever preceded another journey into the prairies.

He had asked, simply, for men who were young and strong, good shots and riders, and experienced in the ways of Indians and animals on the plains. He wanted these men for one month and offered them not a penny of pay, only a vague promise that they would come to wealth if they followed his guidance.

He stipulated with each adventurer who came to him that a tenth part of any loot or possessions that were derived from the journey should become his property. As for the goal of the journey, he had not a word to say.

These words of Galway attracted the curious, and Witherell always was filled with adventurous young fellows who were ready for any sort of excitement. At first, a mere handful would enlist, taking Galway's solemn oath in the presence of others — an oath never to leave the expedition and to stand by the companions of the journey to the death. But when the town saw that Galway was buying five strong covered wagons for the inland voyage, together with horses and mules enough to pull the loads, the village grew more interested.

For those five wagons were loaded with all sorts of necessities, and particularly with lead and gunpowder for the twenty-five excellent new rifles that Galway had bought. It was clear that in this expedition fighting might be expected — fighting and digging, since there were plenty of shovels and picks. But the rest remained a mystery and for the very sake of the mystery the best men came forward to join the little army.

Exactly twenty-four men were chosen by Galway from the volunteers. He made the twenty-fifth.

Only one purchase was made in total secrecy, and that was wood to make a number of sluice boxes. The rest of the buying was public knowledge, and the entire town of Witherell turned out to watch the expedition start. From the side of the river, where the two stacks of the riverboat rose high into the air, the column of wagons and riders started through an outburst of cheers.

Every man had a long rifle balanced across the pommel of his saddle, and nearly all of them carried revolvers, too, and long knives in whose use they were expert either to take the hide off a buffalo or to slash the throat of a man. They were a wild lot. The oldest of them was under thirty, although a good many wore beards that made them seem experienced men of middle age. The youngest were still in their teens, but strong and mature and eager to make up for youth by a more savage daring.

On the whole the men of Galway were perfectly fitted for fighting Indians because not one of the tribes could have picked out a group of men more desperate, more fierce, more totally wild. Many of them already had been outlawed in cities farther

East; the rest had drifted West in the knowledge that the open frontier was the place for them to use their wits and their hands.

Charlie Galway, as the train wound up through the hills away from the town, looked over his outfit with a sort of grim pride. He felt that it was a perfect tool, and that his was the perfect hand to wield it. He felt, also, that sudden elevation of mind that comes to a man who is about to make history. He had not a single regret or shame.

His word given to Sabin did not weigh on him in the least. Sabin was too much like an Indian to count. The red men had to go down. The wave of "civilization" had to wash deeper into the land, deeper and all the way across it, to the western ocean.

So the train dipped down from the hills into the green plain and moved steadily across it like a great, unjointed, but living snake.

All was done in good order. Ahead of the main body three of the best shots on the best horses felt the way. Three more on either side guarded the flanks in the distance and a third trio hung in the rear. It would have been hard to surprise an organism whose nervous system extended so far on all sides. But in case of a sudden attack, at least once a day Galway had his men practice the classic defense maneuver of the plains. At a blast of a horn, the head of the procession turned to the left. The rear of the train pulled out in the same direction, and the five wagons rapidly formed in a circle, like a caterpillar coiling head to tail. Inside that wall men and horses gathered. In Galway's mind, a hundred Indians hardly would dare to attempt the storming of such a place of strength.

They were two days out before the first sign of danger appeared. Then, on the edge of the sky, appeared a little column of half a dozen riders. The bend of their backs proved that they were Indians, riding with shorter stirrups than white men ever used. One glimpse of them was enough to send a thrill through the nerves of the hundred men from Witherell. And after that, all of the wagon train kept a sharp look-out.

Scouts began to come in at least once an hour to report that Indians were visible to right, to left, before, behind.

Well before the wagons pulled through the narrow mouth of the Sacred Valley, there would be fighting, of course. Galway knew that, since the Cheyennes never would give up their holy land without a struggle. But he felt equally certain that the Indians never would be able to guess the destination of the train until it was almost at the mouth of the valley.

If they attacked as the whites entered the ravine, they could be beaten off, no doubt, and, once inside, half a dozen rifles could securely plug the mouth of the gulley and keep a whole world of Indians outside. In the meantime, there would be plenty of food and water within the Sacred Valley, and there would be plenty of occupation in washing the gold from the soil.

The patience of the Indians would finally end. And at last the laden wagons — wagons more preciously burdened than any that ever had rolled across the green of the plains — would come streaming out and pass back to Witherell and a high carouse.

The more Galway contemplated his plan, the more perfect it appeared to him. He could see no possible means of failure, unless the Cheyennes actually managed to make a surprise attack. That he did not expect. As a rule the Cheyennes kept on good terms with the whites, and, although they were keeping the wagon train under close observation, it was unlikely that they would fight unless they were grossly offended.

For that reason, Galway gave the strictest orders that no attempts should be made against any of the Indians who skirted the course that the train was pursuing. That was why a wild rage rushed up into his brain when he heard a chorus of exclamations from the men who rode beside the wagons.

He was inside the powder wagon at the moment, broaching a keg of the stuff in order to replenish some half-empty horns, but, when he heard the men crying out that Jerry Pike was bringing in a captive Indian, he was out of the wagon in a storming temper, at once.

And there, sure enough, he saw Jerry Pike coming with a captive led on an Indian pony beside him. It was only a girl. When Galway made sure of that, half of his anger left him at once. He even smiled a little.

Jerry Pike waved his hat and shouted from the distance. He came up, yelling: "I got a Cheyenne girl for you, boys, and a right pretty one, at that! Take a look at what I found running around loose on the prairie, Galway!"

The captain took that look and then shouted in his turn. "Jerry," he said, "d'you know what you've done?"

"Sure I do," said Jerry. "I've caught a beauty and I'm gonna keep her. I'm gonna make a squaw out of her. I've hunted far enough to find my woman. This is her."

Galway shook his head. "She goes along with us, but she doesn't go as a squaw. Pike, this is Blue Bird, and she's about the biggest medicine that the Cheyennes have. They'll never dare to lay a finger on us while we have Blue Bird . . . . How did you find her?"

"Why, I seen an antelope up the wind and I figgered that a snack of antelope meat would be right good, so I slicked off my hoss and got into the tall grass to stalk. And on the way I come onto a little hollow where a pair of girls was hiding out . . . a white girl and this one.

"The white girl got to her mare in time to run. But I snagged this one and brought her back with me. She looks better than venison to me. *Hai* . . . Cheyenne . . . Blue Bird . . . whatever your name is . . . . How about you being squaw and Jerry Pike'll be heap big warrior, eh? Her brain's gone to sleep, Captain. You see the wood in her face and no sense at all."

"Leave her alone," said Galway. "We're going to wrap her up in cotton and treat her fine. I tell you, she means the kind of luck we've all been looking for. Understand? Blue Bird, you're as safe as you can be. Don't worry a mite about anything. Who was the white girl along with you?"

Blue Bird turned an expressionless face toward him, her eye remained perfectly dead. He was no more to her than the distant edge of the horizon.

A crowd had gathered around them, riders and men on foot, prying at the beauty of the girl with keen, animal eyes.

Galway made a brief speech, but one that was to the point. He said: "Boys, we're in Cheyenne land, now. And you know what that means. The Cheyennes are gonna be pretty sour when they find out we've taken Blue Bird, and they're gonna come swooping down in a flock around us.

"But they won't dare to touch us for fear we'll take it out on Blue Bird. You know what she is? She's the only living Cheyenne that ever was in the Sacred Valley. She's as holy as church on Sundays, to the whole tribe. She's the one that brought them the water in the big drought. If a man touches the hem of her skirt, he has luck for a year. Mind you, now . . . no foolish business."

"I go and find her and then you take her away from me," said Jerry Pike, scowling. "What do I get out of this, anyway?"

"I've got a brand new six-shooter Colt for you, Jerry," said Galway.

"Have you?" shouted Pike. "Gimme it, then. I'd rather have one of them new guns than a whole tribe of squaws."

Chapter Twenty-Three

The blood-red mare whipped Maisry away from the long reach of Jerry Pike, and right across the prairie in a red flash the mare bore her. Three dizzy miles of sprinting, and then the horse stopped, down-headed, utterly winded by that wild effort. And not until then did Maisry's mind clear.

She could think of Blue Bird, then, with a sudden regret that she had not been able to help her companion. She pulled at the hanging head of the red mare and looked back, and before her she saw half a dozen Indians jogging their ponies casually toward her.

Fear slid with her breathing down her throat, nauseated her; she was helpless. She could feel the tremor of utter fatigue in the body of the mare and knew that the knees of the bay were quivering. She could not run. She could only remain there in the saddle and study the danger as it developed before her. Even if the mare had been fresh as the morning, it seemed to her impossible to escape from the wild-headed, light-limbed Indian ponies.

As they came closer, the mare lifted her head and snorted with fear. There was a last terrible temptation to flee no matter how spent the mare might be. That temptation she fought down.

All Indian braves at all times, she knew, were dangerous. But these warriors were painted for the warpath. The streaks of paint — yellow, red, blue, black, purple — robbed them of all human semblance. They were Cheyennes. She could be grateful that she spoke that tongue. The slowness with which they approached

151

gave her a greater hope still. But as they came up, they were pointing her out to one another.

She threw up her right hand in the Indian gesture of greeting. "*Hau!*" she called out, and rejoiced that her voice was strong and steady.

They gave her no answer. They came right on. A young brave, the youngest of that terrible group, said to the others quietly: "I first saw. The scalp is mine."

"That is the law," said the oldest of the group.

The youngster stopped his pony close beside Maisry. The pony was smaller than the red mare, but the bulk of the warrior made him tower above her. The oily paint glistened like blood of many colors on his skin. Moccasins and a loin strap were his only clothes. She breathed, faintly, the peculiar odor of a sweating Indian.

He pulled from her head the wide-brimmed straw hat.

"Look," he said to the others. "This would be a scalp worth showing. It is bright. It is bright enough to shine by its own light."

He thrust his hand into the hair. Unknotted, it flowed down her back, a shining ripple. Still she could speak steadily. It was as though another voice were coming from another throat.

"I am not an enemy," she said. "I belong to one of your people."

The young brave, knife in hand, freshened his grip on her hair.

"You belong to one of my people. You belong to Walk By Night. His hands are on you. Ay, you belong to a Cheyenne."

"I am not your woman, Walk By Night," she said. "I am the woman of Red Hawk."

"*Hai!*" exclaimed Walk By Night. "Red Hawk never took a squaw. Why do you tell the thing that is not so?"

"He has sent for me, and that is why I am here," she answered.

"He is a ghost! He is dead and a ghost!" exclaimed Walk By Night. He began to laugh. He turned his head toward the others, still with that braying laughter. "She says that a dead man has sent for her? Do you hear?"

"It is true. He is not dead. He lives in the Sacred Valley," said the girl.

Walk By Night lifted his hand and moved the knife so that it flashed in her eyes. The hand lacked the little finger, a sacrifice to the Sky People to bring luck and scalps on the warpath, perhaps. It was a big hand. The wrist tendons stood out in great cords under the pull of the forearm muscles.

"Call to Red Hawk now, and he will save you if you belong to him," said Walk By Night. "A ghost can come quickly. Call to him. When I see him, then I will believe."

"Wait," said the oldest of the warriors.

Walk By Night turned his head.

And the senior continued: "Who can tell? She has eyes into which a man can look a long way. Such women are not liars. Think of this, Walk By Night . . . if she truly belongs to Red Hawk, what will happen to you if you kill her?"

"Why should I fear a ghost?" asked Walk By Night.

"We know what that ghost did only a night ago," said the brave. "You saw the Pawnee lying dead with two long gashes in his body. If you kill this woman, perhaps we will find you one morning with the owl feather in your hair and death in your body."

Walk By Night let his grasp fall from the hair of Maisry. He sighed. "If I had that scalp tied to the end of a lance, it would be a fine thing to see the hair blow in the wind and shine in the sun. It would be better than the counting of ten coups to have a scalp like that, Spotted Dog." His eyes shone covetously.

Spotted Dog reached out his brawny arm and stroked the sleek long hair. Because of his words, the girl looked at him with the slightest of smiles. He suddenly ceased to be terrible to her.

"Yes," said Spotted Dog, "it is a very fine scalp to take. Black Antelope had one years ago. It was sacrificed in the time of the great sickness. But if I were you, I would wait until I had made a little more sure about Red Hawk. Lazy Wolf told me once that Red Hawk was to take a squaw among the white people. Perhaps this is the woman. Running Elk will know what to do about her. He will make medicine and find out what to do."

"*Ai, ai,*" said Walk By Night. "Shall I wait for that?" He drew out the hair to its full length, holding it up in the sun. "Look!" he said. "It is like fire. A handful of cool fire. I never saw anything so beautiful."

"Well, it will stay on her head and not disappear," said Spotted Dog. "No one will steal her away from you."

"That is true. We'll go back now to the others."

As they rode, it seemed that a sort of homesickness, a pathetic yearning was in Walk By Night. He could not look on the hair of the girl without mournfulness coming into his eyes.

And so hope kept growing up higher and higher in the breast of the girl. It was not a real expectation that she might keep her life, but she was able to breathe without having that strangling hand of cold shut down upon her throat.

The mare, thoroughly recovered, was ready for running now, but there was no chance for Maisry to slip away and flee from the party. Walk By Night prevented that. As a sign of possession he had tossed the noose of a rawhide lariat around her and rode with the other end of it tied to the pommel of his saddle.

So, as the evening came on, they sighted first the water of a small stream where the horses were allowed to drink, and afterward the little scattered encampment of the war party appeared.

The numbers of the men amazed her. Twenty Indians or so were all that went out on most expeditions, but here there were hundreds who raised a murmur and then a cheerful shouting, as they saw the prisoner brought in.

The encampment itself was merely a circle of saddles and a few meager blankets or light buffalo robes. In the center of the circle the ground had been dug away to serve as a small fireplace, but no fire would be lighted until after dark, of course. In the meantime, the warriors smoked their pipes, chewed parched corn, and ate more than half raw the game that was brought in by scouting parties of hunters from time to time.

It was an uneasy body of warriors, since the sight of the ghost had stopped them abruptly on the warpath. A ghost that passes and leaves behind it the body of a dead Pawnee with the sign of Sweet Medicine attached — such a ghost should be heeded, surely.

But old Running Elk would not definitely turn back from his great adventure; he would not give up the hope of commencing a war with the whites. Ruin might come to the Cheyennes in the long run from such a conflict, but in the meantime Running Elk might remain the head of all the warriors. And the old man hungered for power and glory with a terrible appetite.

When Maisry was brought before him, she found herself looking at a face that seemed, at first, decades too young for the withered body beneath it, but, when she was close, she could see that time merely had dried the face in smooth surfaces instead of in wrinkles. There was the hard, brittle look of a mummy about the medicine man. It was almost strange that he could part his lips without cracking them.

"Here, Running Elk," said Spotted Dog, "is the woman that Walk By Night saw first, and therefore she belongs to him. But she says she is Red Hawk's squaw."

A gleam of brilliant malice brightened the old eyes of Running Elk. That brightness stabbed the hope of Maisry and left it dead.

"What am I to do?" asked Running Elk. "I ask you if ghosts have squaws?"

"Ay, but Red Hawk never was like other people. This woman says that he is no longer dead. She says that he is living again, in the Sacred Valley . . . and she says that he has sent for her."

"How did the message come?" asked the medicine man.

"Blue Bird brought it," said the girl.

Running Elk narrowed those prying, brilliant eyes again.

"You say that Blue Bird rode all alone, all the way to the town of the white men and gave you that message?"

"Yes. She brought it to me."

"Why did she do that?"

"She wanted to call Red Hawk out of the Sacred Valley to stop the Cheyennes before they began to fight with the white people."

"Did she know that Red Hawk was inside the Sacred Valley?"

"Yes."

"*Ah hai!*" cried Running Elk. "Then why did she not call him out herself?"

"Because he would not come to her . . . but she thought that he would come to me."

Running Elk picked up a light robe and pulled it over his shoulders and up like a hood over his head. Through the shadow of it he kept peering at the girl. The sun was almost down. The western light gilded his dry, hard skin. He seemed to be smiling, but his good nature was sheerest illusion. She could feel his hands reaching for her life.

He said: "Walk By Night, give me some present, and then I shall try to find out the truth."

"Here," said Walk By Night. "Here is the horse on which she was riding. It is only a mare but it looks like a fast runner. The color is good."

"The color is very bad," said the medicine man. "See how it flashes. It can be seen for miles away when the sun strikes it. However . . . I shall accept it."

156

He waved his hand and called one of the youths who attended the warriors on the battle trail.

"Take this red mare," he said. "It is mine. Drive it down the creek to the place where my horses are grazing. Keep them away from the rest of the herd."

The lad took the red mare and led it away obediently. And the mare, as it walked off, pulled back and whinnied after its mistress.

Tears came into the eyes of Maisry. She winked them out again and saw the mare disappear over the edge of the creek bank. Hope was gone now. She turned back with a stony sense of despair to watch Running Elk make medicine before the eyes of the warriors.

He was doing the simplest of all rites. He was merely making a circle on the ground, and then, standing inside it, he picked up a handful of dust and blew it away, leaving a few glittering little specks of rock in the palm of his hand.

He lifted his head and said quietly: "Sky People, if I am wrong, speak to me. If the truth lies in the message of the little stones in my hand, be silent." After a moment he lowered his head again, tossed away the tiny pebbles, and deliberately dusted his hands. "The medicine is true and strong and good," he said. "It tells me that she has said the thing that is not true. She is yours, Walk By Night. Sharpen your knife and take off the scalp cleanly and neatly."

Chapter Twenty-Four

The lad who took the red mare down the creek to the rest of the horses that were reserved for Running Elk — a band of half a dozen chosen ponies — hobbled the bay and turned her loose to graze with the rest. When she tried to get away and turn back toward the encampment, the lad tethered her to the lariat of another horse.

He had just finished this work and was about to return to the warriors on the run when he saw a miracle before his eyes, toward the west. He could swear — afterward he did indeed vow — that at one moment there was nothing, and the next moment out of the dazzle of the sunset appeared the form of Red Hawk on the great White Horse.

It might have been explained that the bank of the creek wound around a sharp elbow turn at this point, but to the young Cheyenne nothing would ever dim the terrible splendor of that miraculous happening. He fell flat on his face, groaning: "Mercy, Sweet Medicine. Be merciful! Red Hawk, do not turn my blood to water. Do not draw the living breath out of my lungs. Do not stop my heart. Let me live! Do not take my spirit away to ride with yours in the Happy Hunting Grounds."

Above him he heard a quiet voice saying: "You shall not be harmed. I bring you nothing but good fortune. But tell me what one of the braves owns the red mare you brought down the creek? I only have seen one other like her. Who is her owner?"

"Running Elk is her owner, Red Hawk!" gasped the boy.

It seemed to him that a darkness was coming over his eyes, that he was dying. His breath was failing, too. But it was merely the dying of the sunset and the choking hand of fear that made the difference.

"From whom did Running Elk get her? From some white trader?" asked Red Hawk.

"Walk By Night captured a white woman who rode this mare . . . he has just brought her into the camp. He has not even taken her scalp yet . . . ," said the lad.

And then — he swore afterward — thunder rushed past him. He breathed dust. He saw fire struck out of the rocks. And when his wits returned, the great White Horse and the rider both were gone. There was only a thin mist hanging in the air. A mist of dust? The Cheyenne boy never would believe that. He would swear that Red Hawk had disappeared in a flash, to reappear again, as suddenly, in the midst of the Cheyenne camp.

For no man had an eye behind him, in that encampment. In a dense circle the warriors had gathered to watch the killing and the scalping of the prisoner. It was a thing they had seen often enough before, but the relish of it was never off the roots of their tongues.

Walk By Night was in no hurry. He enjoyed the center of the stage, being a young brave who had counted only two coups in his limited experience. He ran his hand over the face of the girl and said to those around him: "Look, brothers. The white girl is not made like an Indian. The skin is thinner. It is so thin that it would hardly keep out the rainy weather. Her throat is so soft that I could crush the windpipe like that of a young goose, between my thumb and finger. Shall I kill her that way and let her kick and choke on the ground? Give me good advice. There is no reason why she should die too quickly. She ought to take many steps, going to the world of the spirits and not jump off the earth at one step."

Running Elk said: "She is about to faint. After that, she would feel nothing. Cut her across the face and see if that will bring back her senses."

"Good," said Walk By Night, and, taking her by the nape of the neck in one powerful hand, he lifted the hunting knife.

That was when the voice shouted suddenly, and, as the warriors turned, amazed, they saw Red Hawk on White Horse pressing straight in among them. A wild outcry broke from their throats, terror in every voice except that of Running Elk who shouted: "Strike the knife home! She is yours, Walk By Night!"

But Walk By Night had dropped on his face, crying: "Red Hawk, be merciful! I thought she lied . . . I did not know she belonged to you!"

Sabin slipped from his horse. He had seen Maisry throw up her arms, but the wild cry of hope stopped in her throat as though a blow had ended it. He was in time to catch her as she fell and he stretched her on the ground. He pressed a hand over her heart and felt it throbbing, so he was able to draw breath. And his hand still felt that reassuring pulsation while he looked up at the faces around him.

The braves were stretching out their hands toward him, gingerly touching his clothes, his long hair. And as their trembling hands touched the real substance, they began to exclaim: "It is he! He went into the Valley of Death, but he is not dead! He is not a ghost."

He remained on one knee by the girl, saying briefly: "Stay back. Let the wind reach her. Walk By Night, stand up. I am not angry with you. Running Elk, you withered dog, I see the hate in your face. You have done this! Did she not use my name? Did she not speak of me?"

"She did," said many voices.

Walk By Night exclaimed again: "She said she was your woman! I brought her here and Running Elk made medicine that proved that what she said was not true. I would not have touched your woman, Red Hawk. Be merciful. Do not speak to Sweet Medicine against me!"

"If he spoke, he would not be heard!" shouted Running Elk. "What are you doing, staring like foolish men? Did not Sweet Medicine tell us once to make a sacrifice? Why has he come back to us again in the flesh? To be sacrificed again! To give his blood again! It is the will of Sweet Medicine! I hear the voices of the Sky People! He is ours for the sacrifice! Put hands on him. I give the command. I use the words of the Sky People as they sing in my ears! Walk By Night, Spotted Dog . . . all of you seize on him or I shall wither your right hands . . . I shall make such a medicine that . . ."

Sabin stood up, with one downward glance at the pale face of the girl. And she, regaining her senses, began to push herself up into a sitting posture, so that she seemed to be groveling against his knees. Half between sleep and waking she heard him thunder: "Are you men? Are you my people, or are you yelping dogs?"

"We are not your people. Your skin is white. Your soul is white. Sweet Medicine gives you to us."

A dozen tentative hands were reaching toward Sabin. He shouted angrily: "Shall I give you a sign? Shall I bring the god out of the air? Sweet Medicine, appear!" He threw up his right hand high over his head. His whistle sounded piercingly.

And the startled Cheyennes, looking up in turn, saw a huge night owl, greater than ever they had seen before, sweeping down from the sunset sky, sweeping straight down upon them with reaching talons outstretched.

A howl of terror burst from the crowd. From the noise the owl rebounded and left on the ground that mass of warriors in prostrate heaps, and Sabin standing among them with both his arms uplifted.

He said: "Why should I speak to the god for the sake of a worthless people? Why should I intercede for the Cheyennes when the braves are willing to follow an evil old man whose brain is dead except for the planning of wickedness. It was he who persuaded you to drive me out. Running Elk then put his spells on the body of my friend, Standing Bull. So he made himself a great man among you, and like foolish children you followed him.

"But the mercy of Sweet Medicine was very great. First he punished you with drought to open your eyes to wisdom. But when you came yammering for mercy, begging for water, I prayed to the god, and he taught me what to do . . . and water was sent to you. Rain came afterward. But why should a god be merciful to such a stupid people? Now he sends me among you again. Sweet Medicine, hear me. It is I, Red Hawk, standing among these foolish people, whose faces are on the ground. See them, pity them, forgive them for my sake." He drew a great breath. "That is ended," he said. "The wrath of the god is removed from my heart. He is more pitying than wrathful. You may lift your faces again. You may rise. Walk By Night, I bear no evil feeling against you. Rise, every man. Let the horses be caught and saddled. I shall tell you in what direction you may march. And let no man listen again to the snarling of Running Elk. Running Wolf he should be called . . . Running Dog Wolf, old, and only with a tooth to bite fools. Obey my orders. Prepare for the march. I go off to let my anger cool and my heart grow smaller. I go to pray to Sweet Medicine to give more wisdom to his people. . . ."

He drew up the girl to her feet, and then turned and walked out of the crowd.

She, still dizzy of mind and weak of body, saw all things unsteady and reeling before her. But through the dimness of the sunset she could see the terror only gradually fading out of those grotesquely painted faces. She could see them getting cautiously to their feet as though filled with fear.

But they drew back from before her as she walked after Sabin. They drew back as though she were a living flame. They stared at her with great, haunted eyes, and on all sides she heard the frightened, subdued, bass murmuring prayer: "Sweet Medicine, be merciful."

It seemed to her that Rusty Sabin was a giant among men as he strode on.

The great White Horse followed him faithfully. Never once did he look behind toward the girl but, as an Indian chief should do, advanced with his head high, unaware of the world behind him, facing the future. She felt that she was, in fact, his woman, and went meekly behind him.

Chapter Twenty-Five

Word came in to Galway on the run from a galloping horseman. Far ahead, the leading scouts had been met by a deputation of Cheyenne Indians, including one fat, bearded white man who acted as interpreter. The Indians wished to know why the whites were in their territory, and where they were heading. There were two or three hundred warriors on the warpath and it seemed advisable to go with care.

Galway simply said: "I'll go out and break the bad news to them. I'll let them know that we're traveling with a hostage along with us. Eh, Blue Bird?"

He turned and looked at the Indian girl. She sat on the driver's seat of a big wagon and turned an impassive face toward the speaker. But big Charlie Galway was accustomed to this indifference and paid no attention to it. He merely laughed.

"I'm going to show you to 'em, Blue Bird," he said. "I think you'll be the charm that shows us through."

He did what he promised. He took ten picked men, with Blue Bird in the middle of them, and rode out to meet the Indians, advancing a hundred yards or more from the caravan. It had coiled into a circle like a sensitive worm, by this time, with ready marksmen, rifle in hand, looking out through the irregular wall made by the wagons. Indians were everywhere, by this time. They seemed to sprout up out of the tall grass in all directions. Their feathered heads showed here and there against the horizon. But the greater mass of them was directly in the line of the caravan's intended march.

Just out of pointblank rifle fire, Galway halted his men, and at once a party of eleven Indians advanced from the throng ahead.

There was a horse litter in the eleven that came on; there was also a rider on a white horse.

Blue Bird cried out softly: "Red Hawk!"

Galway knew enough Cheyenne to identify that name. He turned and gave the girl a sharp glance. "What is Red Hawk to you, Blue Bird?" he asked.

But the girl was silent. There had been that moment of flashing excitement, and now she was calm again and looked at him with the filmed, unconscious eye.

The Indian deputation came on with the horse litter at the side of Rusty Sabin, whose red hair blew aslant on the breeze. They came straight up to Galway's party, but, as they halted, the proud Cheyennes forgot their dignity to break out into a sudden chorus of exclamations. They were pointing — a thing a warrior never should do. It was Blue Bird that they were distinguishing. Only Sabin himself said not a word and gave no sign as he saw the girl. He merely called out: "Galway, the war chief of the Cheyennes is here with me! Standing Bull got up from a sickbed and came out to inquire why the whites were marching through the land of the Cheyennes. What answer have you for him?"

"We're not the first caravan that ever went across the plains," said Galway.

"The others were bound for California and gold," said Rusty. "They carried along women and children . . . they went to make homes. You go out with a great many men and very few wagons. The Cheyennes are afraid that you mean to make trouble."

A huge, emaciated Indian arose from the horse litter and stood beside Sabin. That was Standing Bull. The white men stared at him curiously, for his fame had reached Witherell long before. He looked like a man who should have remained in his bed for a considerable time. But the energy with which he had rallied himself to the field still remained fresh in him. He stood straight, handling a long lance, returning the stare of the white men with a proud interest.

Galway was answering: "Suppose that you and I ride apart, Rusty. We have some things to say to one another."

"This way," answered Sabin, and turned White Horse immediately to the side. He rode twenty or thirty paces from the others and Galway went out to meet him at once, merely saying to his men: "If anything happens, shoot down Sabin. I can't tell you where we're going, but I can say that he already knows. If he tries to murder me, get him out of the way and everything will be easy after that. Without him, the Cheyennes won't be worth a damn. With him, they're about as good as regular soldiers. He showed that a couple of years ago when he cleaned up the Pawnees."

He rode up to Sabin, after that, leaving his men handling their rifles. The Indians, on their part, pretended no concern, but it was plain that the nervous tension was high on both sides.

As he came up drawing rein, Galway said: "Well, Rusty, I didn't think that I'd run into you as far away from the Sacred Valley as all this."

"You are going back to it, of course?" asked Sabin.

"Back to the Sacred Valley? No, we're just out on a hunting trip."

"It's the gold of the Sacred Valley," said Sabin. "Do your men know that?"

"They don't know. What a fool I'd be to tell 'em," answered Galway. "I'll tell you what, Rusty, you're a fool if you don't throw in with us."

"You swore to me," said Sabin, "that you would never come back to the Sacred Valley."

"An oath a fellow takes when it's forced from him don't count," said Galway. "You had a gun on me when I promised that."

"You lied to me then, and you would lie again," said Sabin. "But turn around and go back to Witherell. I can guard the mouth of the Sacred Valley with half a dozen men."

"If you block the way into the valley," said Galway, "I'll cut the throat of your sweetheart, Rusty. I'll cut the throat of Blue Bird, back there."

"Will you murder her? I think you will," said Rusty slowly.

"Why, man," answered Galway, "I saw her walk out of the Sacred Valley about a minute before the water came sluicing through. She had the look of a gal pretty dizzy with love. I reckon she's worth a good deal to you. Take a sentimental damn' fool like you, and she's worth more than all the gold in the valley. Anyway, I make the bargain with you. Turn loose the Cheyennes and send them home, and I'll turn loose Blue Bird and make it a bargain. Block my way into the Sacred Valley and I'll raise hell with you . . . I'll do it by rubbing out the Indian half-breed."

Rusty looked earnestly on him. "I think it is the will of the god that I should kill you now, Galway," he said.

"If you kill me," said Galway carelessly, "I've got my men watching, and they'll load you full of lead. I know you're a fast man and an accurate man with a gun, Rusty. But the sooner I drop, the sooner you go to hell."

"If I can keep the whites out of the Sacred Valley," said Rusty, "do you think that I'm unready to die? *Ah hai*, Galway . . . you must think that life is a very great thing to me."

Galway grew a little pale. He answered: "And after you're dead . . . and me dead, too . . . what hell will happen to Blue Bird? I've kept a lot of trouble away from her since she's been with us, already."

"Blue Bird," murmured Rusty Sabin, and then he was silent, still staring at the incredible infamy of this white man.

"Kind of hurts you, doesn't it?" asked Galway. "I could see the gal fitted into your idea of a female, and you're sour when you see her held up."

"You have prices for all things," said Rusty. "What is your price for Blue Bird?"

"Prices? Sabin . . . don't be a fool . . . as long as we have her, we can get at the gold in the Sacred Valley. Can you offer us more than that?"

"I am more to the Cheyennes than Blue Bird," said Rusty. "If I come into your hands, will you set her free to go back to her own people?"

"Set her free? Exchange her for you? Rusty, do you mean it?"

"I mean it."

"Why, Rusty, you're the chief interpreter of Sweet Medicine for the tribe. They'd as soon put Sweet Medicine in danger as let you be in trouble. You will exchange yourself for Blue Bird?"

"I don't lie, as you do," said Sabin. "I tell you the truth. Set the girl free, and I go in with you."

"I'll do it, then," said Galway. "Will you come back with me now?"

"Yes. Now," said Rusty. "I go to say farewell to the Cheyennes, and then I return."

He swung away on White Horse and galloped back to the place where Standing Bull was now reclining in his horse litter of two saplings bound to the stirrups of a pair of ponies.

Sabin gripped the hand of the sick man. An eye of profound trust and of endless affection stared back at him.

"I go among the white men again, Standing Bull," said Rusty. "This, I think, is the last time that I shall see you. Remember that I am Cheyenne to my last moment. Think of me in times of happiness. Farewell."

He flashed back into the saddle and was away before Standing Bull could grasp the significance of these words and make a protest or any answer. But the Cheyennes began to shout in astonishment when they saw that worker of great medicine, Red Hawk himself, pass carelessly into the group of the white men about Galway.

Sabin heard Galway order: "Turn the girl loose, some of you, and let her go back to her own kind." He heard the words, but he did not see the wink that accompanied them. For the rest, his eyes were blinded by melancholy as he rode on among the riflemen.

He had left Maisry in the safe hands of Lazy Wolf, who had accompanied Standing Bull into the plains to join the war party. It would be grief for her when she knew that he was gone. It would be grief for Blue Bird when she knew that his life was paying for hers. But he felt, with a strange certainty, that he was no more than a price that must be laid down. A white skin and the soul of an Indian, life appeared to him an endless entanglement.

In the grip of that thought, he entered the gap in the circle of wagons and heard vaguely, behind him, the angry shouting of the Cheyennes. At last they were seeming to understand what had happened.

And then he heard Galway shouting: "When you look around for a smart trader, remember me, lads! I've taken out Blue Bird and brought her back . . . and along with her, I've got one that's worth ten Blue Birds. I've got the great medicine man himself . . . I've got the fool of a white Indian. I've got Rusty Sabin himself."

Sabin jerked up his head from the bewilderment of his thoughts and saw that it was true. Behind him, in the cluster of Galway's riders, was Blue Bird!

Chapter Twenty-Six

There was only a single comment from Rusty Sabin. He merely said: "I was born too foolish to live among the whites . . . and my white skin keeps me from being a Cheyenne . . . I am a man of nothing. Only the god will have me. But you . . . Galway . . ."

He jerked the revolver from its holster on his saddle as he spoke, but he was much too late. Big, capable hands grappled his arm and made him helpless; the gun was jerked from his grasp; a lariat tossed over his shoulders bound his arms tightly to his sides.

He could hear the voice of Blue Bird crying out: "Red Hawk, was it for me? Was it for me? How worthless and wretched I am!"

Then her voice ceased. She was being hurried off to the cover of a wagon. A huge shouting arose from all the men inside the laager. There was laughter and a joyous uproar; many shouted praises of Galway.

And in another moment the order was given, and the wagons began to move forward. They roughly maintained their circle. Outside of them, the Cheyennes swept down in charge after charge, never driving the shock home because they knew that, in case of an attack, both Blue Bird and the greatest of their medicine men would die at once in the hands of the whites. But they had to give some vent to their fury. And so they raged around and around the caravan, shooting their rifles into the air, yelling like fiends.

Far away among the Cheyennes, where Standing Bull was being transported in his horse litter and watching the vain charges of his people, the old, dry-faced medicine man, Running Elk, was shouting: "Now, if Red Hawk is the favored son of Sweet

Medicine, let the god work for him! If his medicine is strong, let him rip apart the circle of the wagons . . . that is easy for a god to do. Nothing is hard for Sweet Medicine."

And inside the circle, Galway was saying to one of his men, simply: "If we try to carry this fellow along with us, he'll slip away. Iron can't hold and ropes can't tie a man with a brain and a heart like Sabin's. There's only one way to make sure of him. Shoot him down and carry the body in one of the wagons until we've come to the place where we're bound."

"What's the good of him dead, when he can be a real hostage living?" was the reasonable answer.

"We'll have White Horse to show the Cheyennes," said Galway. "Who'll do this good turn for me? Who'll put a bullet through the brain of Rusty Sabin? Anyway, it ain't hardly more'n justice. He was likely to've been lynched back there in Witherell. He's only sort of getting what's coming to him. Buck, will you turn the trick for me?"

"Partner," said Buck, "maybe it's good policy, and I guess you're right, but I'd hate like hell to shoot a man that puts himself in trouble for the sake of a gal . . . only a half-breed gal, at that."

"Jimmy, will you do it?"

"Excuse me, Captain. His eyes is too straight for me. I'd have to shoot crooked. My bullets wouldn't hit that kind of a man."

"Then I'll do it myself" said Galway. "Aye, and glad to, at that." He turned the head of his horse and rode straight toward his prisoner.

"Take the lariat off of him," he commanded. "Rusty, you're about to die. White Horse can go on without you. But I won't have you die with your hands tied. Nobody can say that I ever killed a man whose hands were tied."

* * * * *

Blue Bird, in her wagon, stared at the floor with sick, dizzy eyes. There was a smell of salty gunpowder in the air. Black grains of it rolled and jounced like living mites on the boards. And a big keg of it, newly broached, lay on its side.

She looked forward toward the driver of the wagon, and the man beside him. She looked back over the high tailboard. The driver of the mules was lighting his pipe, now, and putting down the box of matches on the seat beside him.

She pulled the plug from the broached cask. There were half a dozen more of those casks piled in the end of the schooner. Now from the mouth of this one a steady stream of black began to pour. She went forward.

A cloud can steal unnoticed across the sky unless it passes the sun. And the hand of a clock moves unseen. But more slowly and casually than that was the drifting of Blue Bird toward the front of the wagon until her hand reached out and slipped the matchbox away.

The striking of the match rasped loudly on her ears, on her nerves. It caused the driver to jerk his head around.

"Hey! Hey! What's up . . . Blue Bird, oh . . . God!" And he snatched out his revolver.

Blue Bird had dropped the match into the wide train of powder. She had intended to make a sacrifice of herself, willingly, not to save Rusty, but because life was worthless to her after he had been betrayed through his fondness for her.

But when she saw the flare of the red burning powder, instinct made her move like a frightened cat. She leaped the tailboard of the wagon and past the noses of the mules just behind. A bullet from the driver's gun whirred past her head. Her feet struck the ground. She ran with all her might as a vast explosion roared behind her, picked her up, thrust her far forward.

She struck with a loose body — like a cat again — and rolled to her feet, still running. Behind her she dared not glance.

* * * * *

Galway had been saying, as he rode at the side of Sabin: "The Indians won't notice the noise. The whites won't tell 'em. And so you'll die for nothing, Rusty. You that have been so damn' big, you'll die like a mouse in the field. Sing out for your god, now. Sing out for Sweet Medicine and see if his medicine is worth a damn when you've got white men around you."

Sabin lifted his freed hands. It was hard to drag the right one past the handle of the long-bladed knife at his belt. But what is a mere knife compared with the interposition of a god?

And he prayed to himself: *Sweet Medicine, look down at me. Here am I among the white men again. But you have not forgotten me. See that with lies and deception they possess me. Therefore show the strength of your hand. Befriend me. Life is not sweet to me. Death would be easy, but for the sake of your own power and your fame among men . . .*

There the sky ripped apart and the earth shuddered. A whole wagon turned into a sheet of red flame. The wagons preceding and following were wrecked. Men were flung flat on the ground out of the saddles. Men walking were knocked over like ninepins.

But both Sabin and Galway kept their saddles. The shock of the explosion made Galway fire a random bullet into the air. He had no chance to fire again, for the gun was ripped from his hand by Red Hawk, and a sixteen-inch blade of steel flashed like a sword toward the throat of Galway.

He threw up an arm to guard his life. But he was late, much too late. The last he saw of life was the strangely cold, calm face of Sabin, and then a red flash of agony as the blade swept through the tender flesh of the throat, deep, deep as the neck bone.

Sabin leaped White Horse through the wreckage of the wagons and rushed out into the open prairie; the dismal outcry of the men of the caravan seemed to diminish behind him, blown away into the past, but before him he saw the slender form of Blue Bird running.

He understood, when he saw her, what had happened, and, slowing the stallion, he called to her. She reached up; she leaped for his foot in the stirrup and he caught her with a strong arm. They galloped on.

"*Ah hai! Ah hai!*" he heard her cry out. "Let me die now . . . now . . . there would be no pain!"

A sweeping charge of a hundred Cheyennes bore raging down toward them, aiming at the wagons. Once arrived, they would make short work of the whites. But Rusty felt a stirring of instinct and blood that made him shout and wave his arm. The charge halted, piled up in a confusion, as he cried: "Let them be! It was the work of the god, not of man. They are in the hands of Sweet Medicine. They will turn back. Do not touch them."

The shouting Cheyennes swerved around and around the caravan, but the word of their worker of miracles was not disobeyed. Not a single charge was pressed home.

* * * * *

As the evening came on, the reformed caravan was seen to turn and begin, slowly, the toilsome march back toward Witherell. With the death of their leader they had lost their goal.

Over the Indian camp, that night, there was a madness of delight. For the scouts kept bringing back word that the retreat of the white men continued. And in the morning the Cheyennes could start back toward their town strengthened by the knowledge that a battle had been won for them by their god alone and the magic of Red Hawk. There was no sad or silent face among them except that of Running Elk, who sat cross-legged on the ground with his robe drawn over his head, unnoticed, powerless, despised by his tribe.

And the happiest of all those groups in the camp was, beyond a doubt, that little cluster of Lazy Wolf, Standing Bull, and Blue Bird, with Maisry among them.

"But now what will come?" asked Blue Bird. "Which of us two, Maisry? Which will he take?"

"Whoever he chooses," said Maisry, "there will be no hate left among us, will there, Blue Bird?"

"No," said the Indian girl. "But what will he do?"

They had to find him first, before they could tell. And he was nowhere to be seen. No doubt he was following with the scouts the train of wagons that journeyed back toward Witherell, to make sure that no mischief occurred between reds and whites.

And then, in the heart of the night, an Indian rode to the little campfire of the chief and spread on the ground his buffalo robe. On the bare hide words had been written in the hand of Rusty Sabin with charcoal.

To Maisry and Blue Bird, to Lazy Wolf, and to my brother, Standing Bull:

Oh, my friends, where I go among you I bring sorrow. The red men sharpen their knives against one another. The white men commit murder. No trust comes to me.

My own heart is divided, for if my right hand held that of Maisry, my left hand would go out to Blue Bird. These things cannot be.

In the west there are tall, blue mountains, and blue is the color of heaven and of peace. I am traveling toward them. If I find wisdom and a quiet mind, I shall return to you again.

Farewell. My heart aches. My heart is colder than a winter morning. To die is no great sorrow, but it is not the will of the god that I should live among you. The red of my heart and the white of my skin have cursed me.

Pray for me. Offer sacrifice. Love one another. Farewell.

Red Hawk
Rusty Sabin

THE END

About the Author

Max Brand is the best-known pen name of Frederick Faust, creator of Dr. Kildare, Destry, and many other fictional characters popular with readers and viewers worldwide. Faust wrote for a variety of audiences in many genres. His enormous output, totaling approximately 30,000,000 words or the equivalent of 530 ordinary books, covered nearly every field: crime, fantasy, historical romance, espionage, Westerns, science fiction, adventure, animal stories, love, war, fashionable society, big business, and big medicine. Eighty motion pictures have been based on his work along with many radio and television programs. For good measure he also published four volumes of poetry. Perhaps no other author has reached more people in more different ways.

Born in Seattle in 1892, orphaned early, Faust grew up in the rural San Joaquin Valley of California. At Berkeley he became a student rebel and one-man literary movement, contributing prodigiously to all campus publications. Denied a degree because of unconventional conduct, he embarked on a series of adventures culminating in New York City where, after a period of near starvation, he received simultaneous recognition as a serious poet and successful author of fiction. Later, he traveled widely, making his home in New York, then in Florence, and finally in Los Angeles.

Once the United States entered the Second World War, Faust abandoned his lucrative writing career and his work as a screenwriter to serve as a war correspondent with the infantry in Italy, despite his fifty-one years and a bad heart. He was killed during a night attack on a hilltop village held by the German army. New books based on magazine serials or unpublished manuscripts or restored versions continue to appear so that, alive or dead, he has averaged a new book every four months for seventy-five years. Beyond this, some work by him is newly reprinted every week of every year in one or another format somewhere in the world. A great deal more about this author and his work can be found in THE MAX BRAND COMPANION (Greenwood Press, 1997) edited by Jon Tuska and Vicki Piekarski. His Website is www.MaxBrandOnline.com.